The Hired Ace

For seasoned gunslinger Reno Valance, trouble is a trade. It's just as well when he reaches White Falls. This place seethes, and soon mayhem reigns. With bullets flying, Reno must act. He'll take a sheriff's oath and his Remington six-gun. Add twenty years delivering the cards of death to bad men, is it enough?

Murder, bank robbery and carnage – Reno must battle all. Amid all this, evil killers kidnap the woman he loves. Can Reno restore order? Can he rescue Anna May? Over two decades he's known only victory. Can he prove again that hell is in the hand of The Hired Ace?

The Hired Ace

Clay Starmer

A Black Horse Western

ROBERT HALE · LONDON

© Clay Starmer 2011
First published in Great Britain 2011

ISBN 978-0-7090-9243-8

Robert Hale Limited
Clerkenwell House
Clerkenwell Green
London EC1R 0HT

www.halebooks.com

Typeset by
Derek Doyle & Associates, Shaw Heath
Printed and bound in Great Britain by
CPI Antony Rowe, Chippenham and Eastbourne

CHAPTER ONE

A man, shouting-drunk, dispatched slugs at the dusk sky as Reno rode in. This settlement – clapboard mostly but with a few structures of stone – was the first township seen in days. Fate had led him there. As he reined his mount off a straight course, the place rose out of a vast grass landscape like a proverbial oasis.

For Reno Valance – 200 pounds of rugged gunslinger, his range gear surfaced with dust, his head shaded by a Stetson – it was a welcome sight. Sore from long miles and with a throat-ache for liquor, a rest was welcome.

These gun antics were not. Many with quick-draw pedigrees had fallen foul of an inebriate's wayward aim. Reno Valance would not be one of them. He perused the thronged thoroughfare. Folk enough crowded those boardwalks, most jeering at the drunkard's tomfoolery. A few moved off, likely mindful of mishaps.

Reno prepared. He cupped the Remington six-shooter strapped at his leg. One drunken stumble, one lurch of that weapon and he'd draw with fatal speed. It wasn't needed though. The drunkard staggered away, his slugs spent, and, sliding off the saddle, Reno touched earth with a grunt of eased tension.

With the horse sated from a trough and now hitched, Reno sought a saloon. It was the Branded Steer – a size-able joint both brimful and noisy. The clientele crowded the length of the long counter or sat relaxed at the Steer's scattering of tables. When a gap opened at the bar, Reno took it and was face to face with a stout-bellied purveyor.

The man smiled. 'Howdy, feller.'

'I've a taste for whiskey,' Reno rasped. He pushed back the brim of his Stetson. 'Say, mister, where the hell I got to?'

'Why, this is White Falls,' responded the barkeep, his words thick with surprise. 'You sayin' you didn't aim here?'

Reno shook his head. 'I've just left them plains. I've been so long in a saddle my brain's fair mashed with it. I'm not sorry for being here, mind.'

The barkeep poured a measure of redeye and deposited the bottle. 'I'm Walt. Listen, friend, you could get sorry. This town's changed. We had us a crazy fool a while since, reckoned he'd dug fist-size nuggets in hills about eight mile yonder.' Walt shrugged. 'We got swamped. We've had it all since then.'

Reno swallowed the liquor and it felt good. The fiery liquid hit his innards with a warm spread of pleasure. 'Gold, you say?' Reno had seen strikes before. At one, up in Nebraska, after miners had flooded the place, no-goods showed. Drifters, rough riders and profiteers all moved in. 'Seems like you've had trouble set in?' Reno figured.

Walt nodded. 'With that bawdy house and how fiery it gets in here. You must've heard shooting outside?'

Reno nodded a reply then restocked his glass.

Walt shaped to talk more but stopped short. Oaths rent the air as two men traded blows – one muscle-bound feller planting a huge fist into the face of another. The beaten drifter slid to the floor, face dressed with blood, where he lay out cold. The fist-winner emitted a raucous laugh and dropped a hand to a holstered Colt.

'What the hell?'

Reno's vicelike grip clamped the man's wrist. The bruiser struggled to break free, but the clasping fingers were immovable.

'You'll stay that gun, mister,' barked Reno. 'You're the second who's sought to loose slugs near me since I touched town. I don't much like it.'

'Who the hell are you to lay law?' snapped back the man. 'Stick in too much and you'll get sorry on it!'

Reno let the man go. 'Now,' he said coldly. 'You're leaving.'

The bruiser's eyes blazed – a million curses in one dark look, and whilst his mouth shaped to an obscenity, he gulped it back. He was defiant though, downing a whiskey in one and slamming the empty glass on the counter top with a bellowed, 'Another!'

Reno sighed. He slid a hand to the Remington. 'Maybe you need your ears dug clean? You'll walk or this'll persuade you!'

The man faltered, his eyes showing his doubt. A moment later, with a dropped gaze he stalked out.

Reno went back to his drink and found another man there.

Nathaniel French had watched it all with growing certainty. Yes, the owner of the Branded Steer was certain all right. Firstly, he'd make a profit that night. More important, he would have this gritty, no-nonsense stranger working for him.

'I'm Nat French. I own the Steer; I card at those tables.'

Reno attacked more whiskey. 'I don't wager,' he drawled. He tapped the butt of the Remington. 'In my line I always win.'

Nat French frowned. 'Can you win against that bottle?'

The whiskey level had fallen a lot. What Reno had drunk could floor a fool but he knew he could take it. 'I hold my drink well enough. Besides, I've got reason to let it settle inside.'

Nathaniel French nodded. 'Troubles, eh?'

Reno dug deep, battling inner demons. Liquor quelled them, sometimes. He came out of his thoughts to see the saloon owner still leaning nonchalantly against the counter.

'Listen, friend,' said French. 'I'll talk some, and after, well, I'll ask but one question.'

Reno nodded. Whiskey began to work its magic.

'I've had them all,' drawled French. 'Fighters and trigger fingers about my tables. My card trade suffers on it. Before talk of gold, I did a steady trade. You wouldn't look to get rich on it, sure enough, but it was a safe deal.'

Reno shrugged. 'Your question is, French?'

The saloon-owner looked grim. 'With drifters and drunks I've got a highly flammable cocktail here. We've had two killings in the Steer of late. White Falls is out of control.'

'I'm jest passing through,' Reno returned.

'I need a man skilled with a gun,' French pressed. 'If I find that man I'll pay him well.' His look was sly. 'My question, feller, is how good are you with that six-shooter?'

Reno recalled the words of an undertaker in Nebraska as he surveyed the bodies of two men in the street: *Why, Mr Valance, you're a real ace with that there Remington. A real ace, yes siree!*

'There's no one better,' he said back earnestly.

'Look,' persisted French. 'If you don't need the money I'll leave you be. If you do need it, and you're my man, I'll pay a darn good price.'

Reno felt for that last twenty-dollar coin in his pocket. He pondered French's offer. The thing was, he'd never worked for another. In the only line of earning he'd ever known, the State paid but you worked for yourself. Your reward was what you caught; or what you killed if they didn't give up.

This had been his life: endless trails, anger taking him on to fell men for dollar bills. You lived rough, you burned under sun and you swallowed dust. You slake thirsts most men couldn't imagine or endure. Now, so much older, he hunted on; he still searched. But new gun-slicks came: younger men, traversing distances at speeds Reno could no longer manage. They were taking his bounty before he reached it. He had hit the buffers and Mexico was his last roll of the dice. Wanted men hid there. It was that last hope.

Next to him, French spoke on. 'If you take up my offer there's a shack at the edge of town and it's yours. We start sundown tomorrow.' French looked expectantly. 'I'd pay your livery fees too.'

Reno thought of the horse. This feller French was crazy but if he was willing to fund a few days' trail break it was fair enough. As for the horse, well, a chance to stand a spell would be reward for her efforts. Reno nodded then. 'I'm Reno Valance.'

French grinned and headed back to his card tables. Reno sipped at his whiskey and pondered on what he'd done. Yet, as he thought more, it dawned that through his gunslinger years he'd ridden to a thousand towns to find nothing but indifference or just plain hostility. He had drunk what his money allowed and ridden on.

Different as this was, he had doubts. After a wandering, violent existence amongst life's dregs, could he settle to anything other? He would give it a go, he resolved, for a while at least. He would see what a spell in White Falls would bring.

CHAPTER TWO

Dawn had broken and, in White Falls's jailhouse, Sheriff Lewis Schaefer considered his deputy. Despite still being in his twenties, Bill Fitz was ready to take the lead role.

'Last night was rough, Bill?' said Schaefer at length.

Fitz sighed, his face grim. 'Hell, Sheriff, you must've heard the shooting? It's so I don't like checking the saloons. You just don't know what you'll—' He stopped short. 'Yesterday,' he exclaimed, a thought striking him. 'It was your anniversary?'

'Yeah,' responded Schaefer. 'Thirty years.'

White Falls's ageing sheriff pondered on wedlock to his childhood sweetheart. Now, one grown-up daughter later and near retirement, last night's celebration should have been a quiet affair. They dined over wine, Schaefer constantly distracted by the gun-sounds outside. He had resisted the temptation to head to Fitz's assistance though. Martha, he knew, was grateful for that.

Schaefer studied his young assistant and remembered

11

Fitz was going strong with Becky Willard. Her folks were strict and wanted a man with some prospects and money behind him. A deputy's wage was hardly the thing with which to woo your in-laws. Schaefer broke the news.

'Bill,' he drawled. 'How'd you like the sheriff's wage?'

Fitz looked confused. 'Say what?'

'I talked with Martha.' Schaefer replied. 'I'm handing in my badge. I'm too old now. It needs younger fellers like you.'

Fitz was stunned. 'Are you definite about this, Sheriff?'

'Hell,' Schaefer gave back, 'I've never been surer about anything. I'm telling O'Hanlon later.'

Fitz was overwhelmed. 'Sheriff, I don't—'

'Oh, holster it, Bill. You're capable and ready.' Schaefer grinned. 'We gotta look for a new deputy though.'

Fitz's blood was pumping as he came to terms with it. He kept his voice steady, saying firmly, 'When you looking to go?'

Schaefer smiled. 'I'll give O'Hanlon a week. I can nigh on smell retirement.'

'Yeah,' Fitz muttered. Realization hit home. He would be head honcho of law in White Falls soon and with the types flooding the prairie town, it was a job with risks attached. He sat there, a man elated and worried in equal measure.

'You awake, Mr Valance?'

Reno stirred, the rattling of the shack door bringing

him out of sleep. He swung groggily off the top of the bed where he'd slept the night fully clothed. He groaned – his head was all pick-axe and pain while his mouth was Texas desert dry. He could take it at night, right enough, but come daybreak he suffered. He approached the door in a haze, slid back the bolt and opened the shack to a flood of light. He shielded his eyes with a hand, swaying a little. A moment later, recovered some, he saw her.

Anna May Gifford was impatient. At thirty-eight and widowed, she just kept busy. This employment with Nathaniel French was part of that. She wore a plain dress with a patterned apron, her hair flowed long, her bright eyes flashed.

Reno battled to settle his own eyes. With all aligned, he liked what he saw. Uncertain of her age – near his own he guessed – he decided she was darn pretty. From his hung-over gunslinger point of view, she looked tough too.

'I'm Anna May,' she said. 'Nat French sent me over.'

'Say what?'

A look of disquiet crossed her face and she pushed him aside. 'It reeks of filth in here, Mr Valance. You slept in those clothes – this won't do at all.' She crossed to the window and flung open the panes.

Reno yawned and scratched his stubble-masked chin with a calloused hand. 'It's a time since I had sheets.'

'Well, now you have,' she said robustly. 'And you'll please to sleep in them. I'll sort you a nightshirt and there's a tin bath out back. I'll boil water and you'll bathe, Mr Valance, d'you hear me?'

He couldn't think what else to say. 'Yes, ma'am.'

'I'll bring a razor and you'll shave and I'll have those clothes to launder.' She studied him up and down. 'I've a mind of your size and I'll bring along pants, shirt and vest.'

Reno shook his aching head. She'd entered his life like a whirlwind, blindsiding him better than any rugged, no-good outlaw. Finally, he blustered, 'Anna May you say?'

'I see to the needs of French's assistants.' She scowled as his eyes widened. 'But get your mind off that!' She bristled then. 'I was brought up proper. You just haul your drink-sodden hide to that bawdy-hole for that.'

Reno smiled. 'Yes, ma'am, and no mistake.'

'This town might be going to ruin,' said Anna May firmly. 'But French's employees will be presentable at all times. Now, let me see.' She nodded abruptly. 'There's an eat-house on Puncher's Row where you'll take your meals, your stabling's paid for, and you've a credit at the hardware for your gun.'

'My gun?'

'What you intending to fire out of it, Mr Valance? Hope and good wishes?'

'Slugs, ma'am; right now I got enough.'

'Get more. In that saloon you'll need them.'

Reno sat back on the bed and just liked her. It was an intuition thing. He'd warmed to men he was about to slay but that was something else. She had an effect that settled his guts and made him ignore the gnawing agony in his brain. He thought of her husband. The poor devil – long since resigned to a life of volley fire instruction.

He asked her straight out, 'You married, Anna May?'

'I was,' she answered curtly. 'But he died.' She waited for a response of sympathy but when none came, she frowned and went on, 'The man had a sickness. He thought he'd seen it through but it came back and took him. I never wed again since. He's buried out at the cemetery.'

'And now you work for French?'

'We both do and that's all we got in common. I'll be spoken to respectful and I'll be here at eight to clean the shack and put on your bath. Exceptin' Sundays when I'm at chapel.' She paused before asking, 'Will you be—'

'Ma'am,' cut in Reno. 'If I walked in there I'd be struck out. Your Lord's an avenging so-and-so, I hear?'

'I'll leave you a copy of the Good Book,' she gave back. 'Even you, Mr Valance, might find some way to salvation.'

Reno considered telling her he couldn't read but decided against it. 'Tell me, Anna May, it seems like you done all this before?'

Her stare was piercing to a man who'd lived so rough and hadn't been ordered about by anyone for this many years.

'Certainly, Mr Valance,' she stated firmly. 'I've already told you, I assist all of Mr French's assistants.'

Reno's eyes narrowed. 'There been many?'

She had a look that Reno couldn't decipher. A moment later, she turned away, disappearing into the room out back which Reno had not yet looked at. She returned in no time carrying a tin bath, which she placed on the shack floor.

'You get the fire up, Mr Valance, and I'll get water from the well. A few buckets will do it. We'll have you scrubbed up in no time.'

Reno couldn't resist. 'You'll be doing that, ma'am?'

She gave him a glare to melt iron. 'Don't test my patience, Mr Valance. When that tub's ready you'll undress alone and pass those dirt-togs through the window. I'll be back in two hours and you'd best be spotless. I'll bring the razor with the clean outfit.' Her lips pursed, then she barked, 'Now, get moving, Mr Valance, a fire if you please.'

Reno found logs, sticks and matches in the back room and soon developed a blaze in the hearth. In no time, with water boiled and in the tub, Anna May retreated to the alley outside the window. He struggled out of clothes sealed on for too long. He shoved his soiled attire out and felt them dragged away.

'Bathe, Mr Valance, get to it.'

He slid into the hot liquid and it felt like a million dollars. It wasn't long before the drowsiness of the fully relaxed began to overtake him. A glass or two or redeye and he would be in heaven.

He considered it all. He was in White Falls – everything provided – and that existence of horse and bedroll over a lifetime of miles was on hold. After so many bad breaks lately, with his ageing bones struggling to make the trails, with those kid-slingers beating him to it, he had ridden to a place where everything seemed to turn to gold.

'You finished in there, Mr Valance?'

Reno shook himself out of his stupor. Time had flown and he stared down at the murky fluid. So much trail dirt had washed off it was hardly believable. A pile of clothes and woollen towels flew through the curtains.

'Remember to take your breakfast at Auntie Ruth's.'

'Anna May,' called out Reno wrapping himself in one of the towels. 'Those other assistants French took on – where'd they go?'

'Go?' she responded. 'Why, Mr Valance, most left as fast as their horses could carry them.'

There was silence then and Reno thought she had left. He reached for the clean clothes as her voice intoned, 'Those last two, though . . . well, they joined my husband in the graveyard.'

CHAPTER THREE

Light receded from White Falls as Sheriff Schaefer poured two whiskeys and proffered one to the over-weight man sitting across the jailhouse desk. Mayor Dennis O'Hanlon took up his glass, sipping between draws on a cigar.

'My mind's made up,' said Schaefer. 'I go in a week.'

The mayor smiled tactfully. 'Now, Lewis, you can't blame me for trying to get you to stay. You've been sheriff in town fourteen years. You'll be hard to replace.'

'You got Bill,' responded Schaefer. 'He's ready, Dennis.'

Mayor O'Hanlon shrugged. 'It should go to a vote.'

Schaefer's annoyance at town process showed on his face.

O'Hanlon, sensing Schaefer's disquiet, pulled the face he always did whenever procedures were being bypassed. 'I'll have to run it by the town council.'

'Hang them,' snapped Schaefer. 'They've seen this town slip and been happy to let it. They figure people make profit but get the wrong people then hell breaks loose.'

'There's talk of writing to the US Marshals' Service,' the mayor gave back. 'Maybe a White Falls patrol atop that; you know – volunteers as back-up?'

'You best discuss that with Sheriff Bill Fitz,' Schaefer grunted. 'Half the men in town don't know one end of a gun from the other; the rest are happy to fire at anything. Get them on the streets together, you'll have sweet carnage, Mayor.'

O'Hanlon nodded his acceptance of Fitz as sheriff. 'OK, a week to get a new deputy.'

'Bill's gonna need a strong hand,' intoned Schaefer. 'Ain't a day goes by without more strangers putting in. Anna May reckons that Nat French took on another assistant.'

O'Hanlon frowned. 'Who's he got this time?'

'I never know any of them,' sighed back Schaefer. 'They're drifters he hires as quick-draw answers if there's war at the card tables. Most hightail when trouble shows but those last two are dead and this new one'll be to bury before I retire, I suppose.'

'French stays safe,' said O'Hanlon. 'He lucky or summat?'

'He ain't stupid,' retorted Schaefer. 'He dives for cover at a hint of bother. It's his assistants that get it.'

O'Hanlon frowned, remembering the details of Tate Holt's killing of the Steer's last hired gun. Witnesses testified that the assistant had drawn first – goaded by Tate – and the killing was lawful. Schaefer was powerless to arrest the fiery youngster. The mayor stood up. 'You'll be missed, Lewis, but you've earned retirement.' O'Hanlon sighed. 'Who's on duty tonight?'

'Fitz again,' said Schaefer. 'God knows who he'll find.'

'It *is* all trade,' said O'Hanlon. 'That suits some.'

Schaefer mused on the fact that a once peaceable community had changed so much. Main Street at night was a rowdy and dangerous place.

'Bill will need help,' he pressed pointedly.

O'Hanlon nodded again. 'Meantime, you'll warn French's new feller? It don't seem a job with prospects, do it?'

Schaefer had already sounded out the person with her finger on the pulse of the Branded Steer's hired guns. He frowned as he uttered, 'Anna May already told him.'

'He's still here?'

'They all reckon they're fast draws,' growled Fitz.

O'Hanlon departed and Schaefer started to build a smoke. He had mixed feelings. With the rate of White Falls's slide, he felt like he was dealing Bill Fitz the Devil's own card.

Reno snuffed out the shack's lamp and headed up the street. He felt invigorated. The clothes Anna May had given him were comfortable but smelt just too sweet. She'd scented the laundry water, he guessed. Even so, a good bathe and a shave and it made a man's mind settle some.

He had eaten excellently at Auntie Ruth's and Reno felt as good as any man could after months of riding rough.

White Falls was busy. Lights flickered in all the build-ings on Main Street and the piano in the Branded Steer saloon pounded out. The boardwalks were full, people strolling by or men slouching across the side rails and talking noisily in groups. No one gave Reno a second glance and that suited just fine. It was as if he was flick-ing a coin, calling heads, and it just kept landing right.

Minutes later he pushed through the Branded Steer's batwings to see a smattering of drinkers. Nathaniel French was in there, his beaming grin sug-gesting he was happy to see his new employee.

'Why hallo,' French drawled. 'You look a new man.'

'Your woman's persuasive,' said Reno drily. 'I reckon as she'll make another man a fine wife.'

French's smirk went south. 'She told you about Todd?'

'If that were his name; she said her first man died.'

French nodded. He'd been lucky to acquire the domestic services of Anna May Gifford. She was much in demand: assistant to Doctor Roberts, regular work for the church in town. 'She cares for my assistants well,' he proffered.

Reno frowned. 'But never for long?'

French shook his head. He was desperate not to lose this hard-man. He resolved to be honest. 'So you know?'

'You said a couple of fellers had been killed in here,' said Reno testily. 'You never said nothin' about them being your men. You ain't been straight with me, I reckon!'

French sighed. He indicated towards an empty table

and they both sat. French had suspected from the first that Reno was in the gunslinger trade – Valance could likely fill a book with the scrapes he'd been in. 'Reno,' he said drily, 'I get fellers raging over a game of cards, or a man dislikes another's face, or it's too many whiskeys. You'll know the score?'

Reno had been to places where only the power of the quick draw mattered. 'You got law in this town?'

French nodded. 'They show now and then. Thing is, in a town size of White Falls it's not enough. I need a feller in here good with a gun for when hell breaks loose. That's why I pay well. Those last two fellers I took on were just too slow. The ones before them didn't have the guts to hang around.'

Reno's eyes telegraphed his interest. 'Go on!'

'We got local problems too,' French went on. 'Couple of cattle outfits – Double D's on one side; Big B's on the other. There ain't no love lost between them. Double D punchers you can talk round. Big B's different. A feller called Holt runs Big B with his three sons. They're all hell-raisers looking for trouble at any turn. It was the eldest Holt boy Tate who gunned down my last assistant.'

'And the one before that?'

'Shot by some drifter who got out fast.' French locked Reno with an imploring stare. 'I chose you because I reckon you can use that Remington.'

Reno nodded. 'Then I'd say you were a right good chooser.' Reno built a smoke. 'I'll definitely be stayin' awhile. It'll get the saddle-sore out and I like the grub.'

'Is that all?' French grinned.

22

'I'm the wrong end of forty,' admitted Reno. 'And I'm feelin' it on the trail. But my draw-hand ain't slowed.' He rose to his feet, stood there every inch the gunslinger. 'You reckon they'll be trouble in tonight?'

French shrugged. 'Most nights it's something.'

'Well then, French,' Reno tapped a finger against the Remington's butt, 'They'll be five aces in any stud poker tonight.'

French was confused. 'Are you suggesting loaded games?'

'No,' Reno snarled. 'Four aces in the pack and me!'

A few hours later, Deputy Fitz downed the last dregs of coffee and listened to the increasing noise of Main Street. Last night had been a shadow of this. Right now, the town's central thoroughfare pounded with sounds of excess – raucous shouts of men spilling though saloon doors or bunching outside the bawdy house. Fitz listened with disquiet to the screeching laughter of girls on the bawdy balcony and bellowed suggestion of cowhands below.

He stood up and instinctively felt for the butt of his Colt. Then, shaking his head at the ferocity of the night's Main Street revelry, he unlocked the rear wall's long cabinet and extracted a Spencer carbine. He picked out a magazine tube from a shelf in the cupboard and inserted it into the gun. He relocked the cupboard, rehoused the keys and prepared to leave. He cursed. There was a new hired gun risking his life for Nathaniel French and Fitz had the whole night to see how that would pan out.

He cursed again. Clutching the carbine tightly, he stepped out to a Main Street that near shook with drink and anger.

CHAPTER FOUR

Reno studied the faces of half-drunk and half-threatening men. With skin bronzed by a life in the sun, their hands calloused by wear and injury, these were the ropers and punchers of the ranches. They wore their holsters low – much lower than any proficient killer would. Still, until the draw you never knew.

Reno watched as French worked the tables. With the saloon reverberating with noise, the pile of bills in the saloon-owner's pot grew invitingly high. Reno felt good. It would be a fair wage for sitting in a wing-back chair all night.

The five-card stud would start soon. All across the West men sweated on what fate – or cheats – dealt. A skilled shark possessed hands that moved cards faster than the human eye. It was odd, Reno dwelled, how more weren't quick-draw gunman as well. Each man to his own, he supposed.

He pondered this again as a voluble party slammed through the batwings. It was made up of four men, all with a rough persona of seasoned punchers, though one looked young. They all bore similar facial features suggesting they were family. This was clearly the Holt clan.

'Beers all round.' The one who spoke was likely in his fifties, overweight and with a full grey beard. 'We got us a powerful thirst.'

Walt drew from a pump. 'Comin' up, Mr Holt. You seared those steers yet?'

'Done it today – all longhorn got the Big B burned on.'

'Don't take much to punch a D to a B,' shouted out a man further down the bar.

One of the Holt outfit stalked forward, his hand dropping to the butt of his gun. 'What you sayin', mister? You accusin' us of mixing your scrawny beeves with our best head of herd? If you're saying we're rustling, why I'll—'

'Steady there, Clem.' Pa Holt moved forward quickly, dragging his son back. 'It'll not be said Big B are startin' a war.' He raised his voice, ensuring all could hear. 'Each caught what's been said about me and my boys: Double D accusin' us of rustling when there's no proof. All heard that I reckon!'

Reno tensed himself to react but after a burst of looks, the two groups parted to opposite ends of the counter. Soon, the Holts took seats at a table. Gradually their voices quieted and Reno could only catch fragments of conversation.

It was enough to map the family though. There was Tate, the eldest of the brothers, blond-haired and boasting a Colt; Clement came next, also packing a .45

26

calibre gun. Lastly, there was the youngest, Matthew, with a Colt at the hip like his siblings. Pa Holt had nothing strapped on.

The night's routine moved on, loud and then peacefully by turns, as drinks were consumed and then more ordered. Voices flowed around the room like breaking waves, often punctuated with laughter and cursing. When the poker commenced, the clock inching into midnight, a couple of the Double D cowboys stepped up whilst Nathaniel French dealt. It was fifteen after midnight when Tate Holt rose from his chair and approached the card players. He passed the steps up to the raised area and threw a glance at Reno as forceful as cannon shot.

French halted in mid-deal. 'You sure you want in on this, Tate? It ain't much of a game.'

Tate slammed dollars on the table. 'Deal me in!'

Reno watched for a while, amused by hostile stares Tate sent in his direction. He lost interest then, settling back on the chair with a contented sigh. Behind him, the piano player continued to pound keys, repeating the tunes until Reno grew sick of them.

Across the saloon the Holts concentrated on their whiskey, the volume of their talk lifting and falling. The rugged others – ranch-hands and nameless strangers propping up the counter – kept drinking too, the noise in that part of the saloon drowning out the talk around the poker table as a constant flow of cards was dealt.

Something drew Reno's attention back to the game. He'd been musing on Anna May but now he turned, to see that the cash pot had grown appreciably. The seats had cleared too, only Tate Holt and one of the Double D cowboys were left in the game. The ambience of the saloon became quieter – the tinkling of the piano keys fading out, sound dying everywhere. Pa Holt and his other two boys rose from their seats to oversee the deciding lay. Reno slid himself up in the armchair. He would be ready.

The saloon's silence was electric, tension holding men rock-still and coiled. It was as if oxygen had been sucked from the room and each person in there held breath until the last card turned.

Tate was called. His three revealed cards were low and that was a worry, but his opponent had the same. Tate turned the ten of spades. It gave him nothing. The cowboy flicked up the jack of clubs. Jack high made the Double D man grin.

The final card turn was started and Tate was first. The king of hearts produced a mummer. King high held the game. Now there was only one card to go.

The Double D man ran his tongue across his bottom lip before unhurriedly, agonizingly slowly to those watching, beginning to reveal what he'd got.

'Show it, damn you,' a watcher shouted.

It was flipped: the ace of diamonds. It made the winning hand!

Tate Holt exploded. He shot to his feet, his chair clattering away behind him and his right hand dropping threateningly to the butt of his Colt.

'You stinkin' cur,' he snarled. 'You scum son of a cheating whore.'

The Double D cowboy remained defiantly calm. He

didn't move an inch, holding his seated position, and his gaze still firmly fixed on Tate. 'That was a fair game, son,' he said firmly. 'You lost it; that's how it goes.'

'That's how it goes?' screamed Tate. 'You load in that ace, Slim Wheeler, and you say that? I been cheated and that's how it goes!'

Reno made the edge of the raised area in two strides. He scanned from Tate to his pa and brothers, assessing the risk.

'Game's done with,' he said firmly. 'You'll saddle on out of here and accept the loss.'

Tate's face was full of rage. 'You said what?'

Reno drilled his stare into the Holt boy. 'I said get on out of this saloon before I make you.'

Pa Holt ran forward. 'No one tells us to get out of no place. Who the hell—'

'A finger twitches,' said Reno, 'and I'll go for my gun.'

Clement and Matthew balked, their hands withdrawn from their gun butts. By now, Tate had swung round to face Reno full on and he was just jittery enough.

'Jest reach for it!' spat Reno. 'That's if you dare?'

Tate's face paled and the look in his eyes said he was unsure. He'd faced and killed French's last assistant but Reno seemed a world of difference. French's new assistant had that air of someone who knew what he was doing.

Tate shook his head at his pa. 'We'll be back.'

'You letting him get away with that mouth?' exploded Pa Holt. 'By God, boy, if I had a—'

'I said leave,' Reno snarled. 'I ain't saying it again.'

Tate Holt backed away, a glare locked on Reno and shoving a table aside as he retreated to the batwings. A moment later, cursing, Tate's pa and siblings followed. All there sensed trouble had been averted, but, close to the batwings, the Holts stopped.

'I got you marked,' shouted Tate, jabbing a finger at Reno. 'You'll grovel. By God, boy, you'll grovel!'

Pa Holt and the two younger brothers crashed out on to the boardwalk. Men pressed to the saloon's edges, leaving clear space between Reno and the loser of the card game.

'Go, son,' intoned Reno. 'Don't be messin' with me!'

Tate's eyes burned and he still held his ground.

Reno sighed and shook his head. And then he waited. . . .

Fitz saw the disturbance at the Steer and he ran fast. Two of the Holt boys were on the boardwalk and their father was swearing loudly. Fitz didn't hesitate. He stepped in, determined to restore order.

'What's this about, Zachariah?'

Pa Holt, his face in rage, spat back angrily, 'My boy Tate's been done out of good money.'

'You got proof, Mr Holt?'

'It were one of them Double D fellers,' Pa Holt bellowed. 'It's that bastard Slim Wheeler. You just look in his eyes for proof of that. Now that scum gun's in there protecting him.'

'I'll deal with it,' Fitz advised. 'You stay out here.'

'Tate, come on, Deputy's here,' cried Matthew Holt.

Pa Holt and his two youngest sons descended the steps and stood in a huddle on the street. Fitz placed a hand against the batwings but a gun blast drove him sideways. He cleared the door's gap before pressing himself up against the saloon's front wall. He set to cocking the carbine but watched aghast when, an instant later, Tate Holt hurtled out of the Steer. The eldest Holt boy fell back with a rigidity that no living soul could achieve. He smacked the boardwalk with a bang, his body bouncing as the worn timbers gave under his weight. Then he lay there with a stillness that left no doubt. If confirmation were needed it was that perfect hole between Tate's eyes. It was a red statement of death.

Chaos reigned: Pa Holt wailed, scrambling with pitiful cries up the boardwalk steps and cradling his slain son. While Pa Holt wept over the corpse of his first born, his two other sons stayed rooted to the street. They, like Fitz, were stunned to a standstill by what they'd just seen.

Fitz pulled himself together. He moved toward Tate's body but drew back as Pa Holt threw up a blocking arm. The deputy glanced at the younger Holts and he guessed what was coming next.

Matthew broke first, rushing the steps, but Fitz quickly halted him.

'Get back!' he barked. 'Leave this to the law.'

Matthew wailed, 'The scum's killed Tate. He's gotta die!'

'Bed that pistol, boy,' Fitz growled, levelling the carbine, 'unless you aim to join your brother.'

31

Matthew's eyes burned but he did as he was told. Clement leapt forward then. He lowered a shoulder and barged at the deputy. Fitz reacted swiftly. He freed one hand from the carbine and grabbed Clement by the shirt collar, bringing a knee up at the same time. He applied force to the young man's mid-riff, doubling him up. Clement slumped down, rolling on to his side, his hands clutching at his stomach.

Matthew Holt moved up to join his pa. Both of them wept and howled over the body of Tate. As the Holt men mourned and suffered in the street, Fitz crashed the batwings.

Inside, Reno held his ground. He stood ramrod straight on the raised decking with the Remington held at his side. Tables were upturned everywhere, men emerging from their shelter. Walt eyed the mess with a groan. Glass fragments littered the floor and sawdust had darkened with the soak of thrown drinks.

Fitz threw Valance a stern look. 'You killed that boy.'

'Boy?' Reno shook his head. 'He was all growed-up from what I saw; from a family of killers is what I heard.'

'Tate's shooting of that feller was a lawful slaying,' growled Fitz. 'There'd darn best be proof on this killing?'

French clambered into view from behind the bar and he smiled weakly. 'It was justified and legal, Deputy. Valance drew after Tate Holt went for his gun. He was given plenty of warning to leave peaceful.'

A ranch-hand from the Double D barked out, 'I saw it full, Deputy. Those Holt fellers had it coming. French is right. Tate pulled on this man and he had to defend himself.'

Fitz was at a loss. Just so had it been when Tate Holt slew the assistant weeks before; with witnesses enough to verify Valance's actions there was nothing the law could do. 'You'll all sign to back that?' he barked testily.

'I'd swear it to any judge,' spat back the ranch hand.

Fitz lowered the carbine and surveyed the carnage. He felt disappointed. He'd lodge the body at the jail until the sheriff came in the morning and he had nothing to pin on Reno Valance. 'There's been trouble enough tonight,' he snarled. 'You'll shut the Steer and I'll get that body moved.'

Walt nodded and threw a rag over the beer pump.

Fitz headed for the door and French grinned at Reno. 'Darn good shooting. I'd say we'll do a power of business.'

Reno listened to the cries of the Holt family outside and he shook his head. He cursed softly. He'd given that fool kid Tate enough chances but he'd kept pushing it. A few times Reno thought Tate would leave but he held by the batwings, hand hovering over the butt of his gun. When Tate lurched for the weapon, Reno reacted with the speed of a viper, dragging up the Remington with the practice of all his angry years. The Remington barked, blazing flame and smoke as lead hurtled out. The slug struck exactly where Reno aimed it: slap-bang between the eyes.

French uprighted a chair and slumped into it. Reno slid the Remington into his holster. Twenty minutes later the Holt family had carried Tate's body over to the jailhouse. They had protested long and loud that they wanted to take him back to their ranch, but Fitz had insisted it was evidence and needed to stay in the jail-house until the morning, when Schaefer came on duty. Eventually, the Holts headed out, with shouts of revenge.

When all was quiet Reno joined French at the table. Walt gave them a glass each and deposited a bottle.

'That's the last of *them*,' drawled French. 'Leastways, they'll not be back tonight. No, they'll break it to Tate's ma.' He paused, drawing out a cigar from his vest pocket. 'I'm hoping this is an end to it. They've been hurt.'

'They'll be back?' Reno muttered. 'I'll be waiting!'

French felt satisfied. This night's work would ensure fewer hotheads frequented the Branded Steer, for a while at least. 'Our deal,' he said at length. 'You're OK with it?'

'Depends,' Reno returned drily. 'What we made?'

French smiled. 'Sixty each. It's a middling sum.'

Reno mused on it. He'd earned bigger amounts in the past but he'd had to hunt hard distances to get it. This was honest and easy dollar, with the promise of more. For the ageing gunslinger reality dawned. He had traversed this land for twenty years; he'd slain for a wage – a slaughterer's pay. He had feared no one; let no one close. Now, worn through and alone, yet his quick-draw skill undiminished, he sought the stay-put existence he once abhorred. He wanted Anna May. He wanted White Falls. This was the end of the road.

French rambled on. 'This is just the start.'

Reno poured another whiskey and downed it in one. He took the bills that French passed him and pocketed them. 'Fine woman, that lady of yours,' he said, an enquiring stare cast at the saloon owner.

'She ain't anyone's lady,' French scoffed. 'She's more ornery than a stepped-on rattler. She's good at the job, mind.'

Reno nodded. 'I best hit the bed. Anna May says I've to be awake at eight. It's a tin bath, a shave and more sweet-smellin' clothes.'

French laughed. 'It's like you're married, ain't it?'

Reno left. If anyone had been listening as he strode along the now quietened Main Street, they'd have heard nothing but his purposeful voice from the saloon door to the shack: 'Fine woman that. Yep, she's a fine woman indeed!'

CHAPTER FIVE

The next morning Schaefer whistled in admiration as he examined the body of Tate Holt on the floor of one of the cells.

'Result of losing a poker hand,' drawled Fitz.

'Well, you can't say it weren't coming,' observed Schaefer. He peered down at the perfect slug hole equidistant between the slain man's eyes. 'Darn me, I reckon from that there piano platform to the batwings can't be less than eighty feet. That's one hell of a shot!'

'It seems Nathaniel French has finally got him a real ace,' Fitz responded. The deputy pushed back the brim of his Stetson. 'The feller goes by the name of Reno Valance.'

Schaefer settled into a chair. 'What d'you make of him?'

'Cool as iced water,' answered Fitz. 'French and the fellers from the Double D backed him up. Legal slaying and that's how I'm writing it.'

Schaefer nodded, glad that for once the paperwork wasn't down to him. After a moment, he asked, 'How did Pa Holt and his other boys take it?'

'There were some cussing and threats,' returned Fitz with a shrug, 'but nothing I'll act on given what's happened. I reckon they were too cut up to go back at Valance.' He sighed reflectively. 'It'll take a mite to sink in, I'd say. Mind you, with Tate dead and their bravado blown, it might make the Holts think twice about causing trouble now.'

'French has got the right man,' noted Schaefer drily.

'You just know that Reno Valance is neck-deep in killing,' responded Fitz sourly. 'He's too steady by half with a dead man to answer for. He didn't blink an eyelid when I challenged him about slaying Tate.'

'Look, Bill, you handled it OK,' praised Schaefer. 'It's been copy-book as far as I can see. You really are ready.'

Fitz resisted the urge to smile. He was still coming to terms with Schaefer's imminent departure, but the praise was welcome. He thought then of the work involved: a report on Tate's death would be required for the drunken Judge Melville.

Schaefer anticipated his deputy's thoughts.

'Melville usually sobers up about this time of the month. Nothing for him to mind here, I reckon. We'll hand Tate's body back to his family and they can sort the burial. When Melville comes through you run the facts by him. An open-and-shut case, as they say.'

Fitz was silent. He mulled over what he'd seen of the man called Reno Valance. Someone who was that calm and who possessed those killing skills had to have a questionable history. At length he muttered, 'You reckon I should look into this Valance feller?'

Schaefer was less than interested. He avidly scanned some documents on the desk, not even looking up as he mumbled back, 'Say, what's that again?'

'Valance?' snapped Fitz. 'Do some checks?'

Schaefer glanced up now. He pinned Fitz with a curious stare, and then laughed. 'You're keen as mustard, ain't yer, Bill? Soon you'll be too busy with paper to be chasing every drifter.'

'I'll ask about anyhow,' Fitz growled. 'Just to be sure.'

'OK, Bill,' Schaefer drawled. 'I got a stack to do and if you want to snoop about Valance that's fine by me.'

Fitz blew out his cheeks. He'd check the livery first. A talk with the owner and a look at a horse could tell him a lot. He crossed to the door.

'You'll go to the Holt ranch?' Schaefer called after him.

Fitz sighed. 'You got to feel for poor Ma Holt, eh? She'll be pining summat rotten?'

'Yeah, tragic,' mumbled Schaefer back at his papers.

Fitz shook his head. He turned toward a White Falls' Main Street morning.

'That's better, Mr Valance.' Anna May looked round the shack approvingly. 'That's so much better, by half!'

Reno had been up in plenty of time. He'd gathered firewood and water was on, starting to bubble as it peaked to boiling. With the windows open and the bed made, the place looked cared for. He was still in the nightshirt she had provided and he felt a twinge of embarrassment.

'This is somewhere you could bring your mother to,' said Anna May with a curt nod. 'Or. . . .'

'Or what?' responded Reno cagily. He suspected something.

'Or the preacher.'

'Say what?' Reno spluttered. 'The *preacher*?'

'I've asked him to call.' Anna May stiffened. 'I heard you shot a man dead last night and your soul's in peril. You need redemption and right fast.'

'My soul,' returned Reno incredulously, 'is booked into Hell, ma'am. Booked in – board paid and for all eternity!'

'It's never too late to be saved, Mr Valance. Should just one sheep return—'

'Stow it, sister,' barked Reno, annoyed. 'I'll oblige you with your tin baths and what not. I'll go here and there smelling like some blessed dandy because you've put some woman's spell on the laundry water. I'll even wear this . . . thing!' He clutched at the nightshirt with one hand. 'I mean, string me up and brand me like a steer if I ever got seen dressed as such.'

She folded her arms across her chest. 'You finished?'

He shrugged. 'I reckon so.'

'You will bathe, Mr Valance. Then you'll wait till I return with the preacher. Then we'll read from the Good Book. It'll be passages of redemption, I suppose, or how a man who's slain another seeks forgiveness from the Lord.'

'I got to say, Anna May,' drawled Reno. 'You're one pushing woman and that's for sure. Don't you ever give up?'

'Women ain't got time to,' she retorted.

Reno shook his head. 'I won't do it.'

'You will too.'

'Darn it, missy,' growled Reno. 'I will not.'

'Swear at me again, Mr Valance, and I'll put that bath over your currently hopeless head. We'll find a passage on redemption and you'll read it to the preacher and me.'

She turned to leave.

'No, ma'am,' he called out. 'That's summat I cannot do.'

She glared back. 'So you're refusing?'

'No,' replied Reno. 'I'm telling you I *cannot* do it. Anna May, can't your stubborn ears hear that I just can't read!'

She had a look in her eyes that he couldn't fathom. Then she left quickly.

They were at the table in the ranch house kitchen. The door was ajar, a scent and sound of beeves heavy in the breeze. Ma Holt wept softly, dabbing at her eyes every so often with a handkerchief Matthew had passed her when his mother had begun to cry.

'Ma,' said Matthew with passion. 'We'll get revenge.'

She looked up, directing a fiery stare at her youngest son. 'You'll get nothin', Matthew Holt, short of breaking my heart more. When Tate killed French's man I knew it would happen. All of you – allus going on about how fine gunmen you are! Well you ain't, you hear me, and this has proved it.'

'So they get away with murdering my boy?' spat Pa Holt.

'Our boy lies stiff and dead in White Falls jail,' bellowed Ma Holt. 'And I blame you, Zachariah.'

'Me? How in hell's—'

'Yes, you!' screamed Ma Holt. 'You got these boys into drinking and playing poker and carrying guns. If they'd stayed on the ranch like I always wanted Tate would be livin' now.'

'We're grown,' protested Clement. 'We find our own way.'

'Your own way,' Ma Holt barked back. 'That'll be a plot six feet long in White Falls graveyard. You've danced with the Devil for too long and now he's bit. French's new gun feller sounds a man hell-quick with a gun. Tate's dead owing to coming up against a fast draw. You face him again and you'll be where Tate's at!'

'Slim Wheeler from the Double D cheated and that gun scum killed our boy,' scowled Pa Holt. 'We can't leave it.'

'Sheriff will give justice,' Ma Holt barked.

'Justice!' cried Matthew. 'That Deputy Fitz were there and let it go by. He made out it were a lawful killing.'

Ma Holt wept again and it was some moments before she regained her composure. 'Eye for an eye, it says in the Good Book. Well, I reckon so. Now it's done and it stays done. No more killing on either side.'

'But, Ma,' bellowed Matthew kicking back his chair as he jumped up. 'We can't just—'

'You'll do as you're told,' roared back Ma Holt. 'Zachariah, you'll hitch up that wagon and go into town. You'll buy a coffin and speak to that preacher

41

about a burial. Then you'll bring my Tate back so's I can say my goodbyes and get him ready.' She stood up, her look defiant. 'They'll be no more killings and you'll stay out of the Steer, now and for good!'

She left the room and Matthew slid back into his seat. 'What we going to do, Pa?'

Pa Holt wore a look of fury. 'We do as Ma says,' he growled, 'for now. We go get Tate and we'll have his burial. When dust settles and Ma comes round we'll make our move.'

'But Pa,' protested Matthew. 'We got to take the gun scum out. We got to put his stinkin' carcass in Hell.'

'How?' snapped Clement. 'Ma's hitched us to the ranch.'

When Pa Holt didn't answer Clement doubted his own statement. 'You reckon you'll talk Ma round? She'll let us go to the saloon again?'

'Whether she does or whether she don't ain't something I got much say on,' responded Pa Holt with hell in his eyes. 'But I got a say on that gun scum and the Double D. They'll die. Believe me, boys,' he spat, slamming his fist down hard on to the top of the table, 'they will die!'

CHAPTER SIX

It was past noon when Fitz got to the Holt place. He clambered off his horse and ran a sleeve across his brow. The day was hot and the few miles he'd ridden out to the Big B ranch had been tough. He let go of the mare's leathers and she instinctively paced the few yards to a horse trough.

Fitz looked around. All three surviving Holt men were out in the fenced yard at the front of the house. All scowled.

'You can collect Tate,' said Fitz.

Pa Holt sneered. 'I'll get a wagon hitched and bring him home. You and Schaefer seen sense over my boy's murder?'

'I got witnesses saying Tate drew first, Mr Holt. It's gotta go down as a lawful slaying. I'm sorry for your loss.' Fitz gave Pa Holt an intense stare. 'Nat French's got him a man handy with a gun. It'd be best, I reckon, to pull in your horns about the Branded Steer.'

'You tellin' us what we can and can't do now, Deputy?' spat Clement. 'You're mighty changeable with the rules. You let someone murder my brother yet you lay heavy on us.'

'Leave it, boy,' growled Pa Holt. 'These laws always took against Big B people. That's the way it is.'

Fitz shook his head. The Holt men had always been difficult to reason with. The patriarch's anger had affected his sons from an early age. Schaefer had once spoken of a spell, a decade before, when Zachariah Holt was less difficult. Over time though, as more family ranches sold out and Clint Drummond's Double D spread expanded, the bearded small-scale beeves man had become embittered. Now, with the loss of Tate, there would be no getting through to them. Still, he'd warned them against confronting Valance and that was all he could do.

He moved to his horse and remounted. 'Schaefer's waiting in town. I hope you'll heed what I said.'

'We'll heed nothin',' screeched Matthew. 'Except. . . .'

Fitz was almost at the gate but he reined the horse still. He looked back intently. 'Except what?'

Pa Holt shoved at his youngest son and smiled. 'Just gettin' poor Tate, Deputy. Now get, hitch that wagon up.'

They moved away and Fitz rode on. He just knew they were set for revenge.

Later that afternoon Reno stood in a walkway and lit up a smoke. The narrow gap between two buildings gave a short-cut access to the back of the livery. He liked to wait there, hidden from view of those passing along the thoroughfare, just observing.

So it was, a few draws on that built smoke later, that he saw the Holt family trundle in on a wagon. He was surprised. It was a muted affair – no shouts of anger or emotionally charged threats. Instead, they carried the body of Tate, wrapped in a sheet, on to the tailboard and then quietly drove the wagon away. As they disappeared from view Reno stamped the smoke into the dust and strode off.

He was determined not to return to the shack. If Anna May was there with her cursed preacher he would get mad and he didn't want that. He really liked the woman, despite her domineering tendencies. It was better to stay out of the way.

He emerged behind the livery and was soon checking on his pinto, turned out with a dozen other horses in the corral. There was no sign of the livery owner or his assistant, which caused Reno to pause. He pondered whether to wait or move on. He wanted to ask about the care of the mare: the animal needed reshoeing, but he could do that any time. He did wait though, leaning over the corral's top bar while thinking hard. He was still there after thirty minutes had passed and an old-timer appeared out of the livery stable.

'Howdy, mister. Your horse's settled right in.'

Reno nodded. 'You'll put new shoes on her?'

The old man nodded. 'Sure thing, feller; so long as French keeps paying she'll be took care of.' The liveryman smiled. 'You plannin' to stay long?'

Reno shrugged but said nothing. The oldster moved off and Reno pondered. The life he had led – endless wandering and hunting down the dregs of men – was finished. These last couple of days, even allowing for the death of the Holt boy, had permitted some settled living. He hankered for more of this. Roots had to be set down sometime. Why should it not be here?

He stopped mulling, resolving to get slugs from the store. He took the alleys back to Main Street and was almost at the boardwalk steps when a voice brought him to a stop.

Reno turned to see the deputy standing outside the jailhouse across the street. 'Valance, a moment please.'

Fitz crossed the pot-holed thoroughfare, making Reno frown. 'I'm kind of busy, Deputy.'

'We've returned Tate Holt's body to his family,' said Fitz matter-of-factly. 'It's written up as a legal slaying.'

Reno shrugged. 'He drew on me; it had to be my funeral or his.'

Fitz forced a smile. 'One hell of a shot you took him out with. Where'd you learn to place a slug like that?'

'You fishing for news, Deputy? Listen, where I've been you got to make it a fast shot and straight. That's about it, or that's all I'm telling you. You won't find me on a wanted and I'm free as the wind and doing a job I get paid good for.'

'You're a hired gun, Valance.'

'No, Deputy, I'm Nat French's assistant. It'd suit me if my gun stayed bedded, but if fool kids like them Holt boys shout their mouths off and wave Colts a man's got a right to protect himself and the man that pays him.'

Fitz nodded. 'Well, I can't argue with that. I suppose I'd better tell you I was at the Big B ranch earlier.

They're spitting bile at you.'

'I reckoned as much,' replied Reno calmly.

'Maybe me and the sheriff should patrol the next night or two,' Fitz thought out loud. 'There could be more trouble.'

'You do what you need to,' drawled Reno. 'I go to work at sundown in the Branded Steer.' He put a foot to the steps but halted as Fitz spoke again.

'Mr Valance, I'm making enquiries about a feller who turned up in town about the same time as you. I don't suppose—'

Reno knew the deputy was lying. 'I ride alone.'

'I was going to ask if you'd seen him about. Tall feller. I reckon as he might have stabled his horse at the livery. Perhaps you've bumped into him?'

'I mind no one,' Reno answered bluntly, 'unless they bother me. Only one feller's done that and he's dead.'

Fitz nodded again. 'Thanks for your time, Valance.'

They parted, Fitz sure in himself that Reno Valance was a man with a dark and dubious past; Reno sure that the young lawman would keep on to him like a dog at a bone.

CHAPTER SEVEN

Time passed, the sun baking the streets by day, the temperature plunging at night. At this moment, way past dusk and a dark sky bringing the lamps on in White Falls, Reno pondered.

Since Tate's death, none of the Holt family had frequented the Branded Steer. They'd been sighted in town though. The previous day Tate's burial had taken place. It was poorly attended, only the family and the preacher committing the man to ground. Schaefer and Fitz stood near by, at a discreet and respectful distance, keen to avoid any trouble.

Reno had watched it from the alley. After the casket was lowered, he'd met Anna May at the shack. She had begun to teach him to read. Abandoning her plan to save his soul, she set to improving his learning. It was slow progress. Reno had not had a minute of schooling and when she'd shown him the alphabet he'd stared at it like it was a hangman's noose. Her patience had been admirable, though, persevering until he began to learn each letter.

Now, as he sat on a chair in the Steer, he just watched for trouble and wondered when the Holt boys would come.

The saloon was busy tonight, the long bar crowded with men and all the tables full. French was dealing cards with a couple of the Double D ranch hands and the piano player pounded on. Thankfully, he'd chosen some tunes to lighten the tedium.

Reno looked at the tallboy clock. The elaborate hands said it was eleven p.m. Moments later, he saw a man wearing a star on his chest push through the batwing doors. Reno recognized White Fall's top lawman from the funeral.

Walt Cooper smiled broadly and called, 'Evening, Sheriff, you're early tonight.'

Schaefer gazed around with some relief. All seemed quiet. 'I thought I'd look in on account of the shooting, Walt,' he gave back cheerily. 'It seems OK in here.'

Walt nodded and moved off to refill a customer's glass.

Schaefer was turning to leave when he sighted Reno. He pondered for a moment; then, curious, he approached.

Reno braced himself for more questions.

The grey-haired sheriff nodded. 'I'm Schaefer.'

Reno nodded back. 'I reckon as you know my name.'

'Well, yeah,' said Schaefer. 'If that *is* your name?'

Reno bristled at that. 'An innocent man's got a right to call himself what he wants.'

'I don't doubt it,' answered Schaefer. 'I can't quite pick your accent, Valance. Where'd you hail from?'

'No place and anywhere; I've been around.'

'You're kinda cagey for an innocent man.'

'My business is my own,' said Reno, sitting up straight. 'I've got to say, Sheriff, right now you're keeping me from it.'

Schaefer frowned. 'Business?' he queried. 'You're a hired gun far as I can see. Mind, I'll grant that you're a good one.'

'Ain't you the same?' drawled back Reno. 'Behind that badge, Sheriff, you're paid to kill!'

'I mind this town,' Schaefer retorted. 'There's more to the law than slaying, Valance.' The sheriff was riled. 'There's a difference between me and an executioner.'

'Assistant,' responded Reno calmly, 'just trying to keep it peaceable in here. I reckon as you would want that.'

Schaefer levelled his temper. He sighed then. 'Well, you're right enough about that for the next few days.

Reno shook his head. 'A few days, you say?'

Schaefer shrugged. 'I retire soon, Valance. It'll be fourteen years. That's a good distance for any lawman.'

'Truly,' said Reno. 'Deputy will be on his own, then?'

'He will until we get a replacement. Fitz is taking the sheriff's star.'

Reno nodded. 'I reckon me keeping it steady in here will be a big help.'

Schaefer frowned. Despite his distrust of the gun-slinger trade, he offered out, 'Someone who shoots like you would be a powerful benefit in a town's sheriff's office. You ever. . . ?'

Reno grinned. 'I got a job in here. I ain't the man to

be wearing a badge.'

'Bill told you the Holts ain't took this killing well?'

'Who would?'

'You ain't worried?'

Reno shrugged. 'If it comes I'm ready.'

'Well, yeah, that's true enough. You just watch your back, Valance. Bill and me will show our faces in here when we can and we'll keep an eye on your shack.'

'Mighty obliged,' answered Reno. 'But I reckon as I can handle whatever shows up.'

Schaefer nodded and turned away. When he reached the batwings he agreed absolutely with his deputy that Reno Valance *was* as cool as iced water. He was calm too, like a man who'd faced death so many times that it became as natural as breathing.

They reined their mounts to a stop by a hideous confusion of trees. Darkness laid its lies on this unknown land. Tracks failed before them; suggestions of structures were unmasked to be nothing but more black sky. They were both on edge, every sense wire-sharp against the potential threats of this vast expanse of cloaked wilderness. Every critter's scratch could make even the hardest man bolt upright in the saddle, reaching for his gun. The mind outlined a myriad of horrors over the miles of dark riding. This was an alien world and they were two men with reasons to worry.

'This blind-ridin' would get a posse off your back,' drawled Silas Tyrell. 'But hell, Jeb, it makes a man think bad!'

Jeb Buffett knew all about bad. At the age of thirty-six, he had racked up enough trouble for the states of Colorado and Utah to want him dead or alive. The bank robberies he'd committed in those jurisdictions had been a means to an end. The men he killed had been merely incidental to his hold-up.

Buffett knew full well what to expect: a noose was waiting and it would only be a matter of time. Whether it came by lawman, a posse or a lynch mob, the result would be the same – strung up from a branch and then kick away. He wouldn't be afforded a fast drop. There would be no broken neck to make the journey to hell a fast and clean one. No, he'd struggle and slowly choke. That was the way for the likes of him. Better to go in a gun battle, Jeb would often advise Silas. Go fast and famous.

The last few months had been tough: harried by posses, escaping unscathed from the attentions of gun-slingers, living rough in places where only the desperate go. Funds were low now. They needed to stock up on dollars and decent living.

Silas, his features obliterated by the night, was a thin, shifty veteran of property crime. Commercial premises or domestic houses, he would give it a go. 'Hey, Jeb, we making camp?'

Buffett barked back, 'Hang it, Silas, we must be close.'

'Eight miles maybe; that feller said south of the hills.'

It was at their last hideout that they'd heard of the White Falls gold find. It was the usual stuff: nuggets as large as your hand; a fortune you could walk on and the town's assay office and bank getting fatter by the day with profit. They knew others would come, drawn as they were by a scavenger nature. There would be mail coaches carrying boxes of dollars out; there would be the bank's stacked vaults. This gold claim was months old and they'd reasoned that, by now, whilst some gap-toothed old-stagers would still be labouring with pick axe and pan in the high ground, the real wealth would lie under lock and key in White Falls.

Silas shifted in the saddle. 'What d'you reckon to us getting some sleep. We'll ride to White Falls when sun's up. My sorry bones are feelin' it.'

'Mine too,' returned Buffett. 'But we're out of redeye and I'd kill me a preacher for whiskey. We'll go on.'

'A bath, a bawdy-house and some beers,' intoned Silas, steeling himself to ignore the pain and struggle on.

'That's it,' growled back Buffett. 'Eight miles more and we've got us liquor and linen.'

'What about the law?' Silas urged his horse forward. 'You reckon as our wanted posters got out this far?'

'Law?' growled Buffett as he forced his mount into a descent. 'I never did kill me a sheriff yet!'

Pa Holt had just about given up hope when he turned in the direction of the Branded Steer. He'd trawled the saloons and drinking dens of White Falls without success. He needed the right sort of man who would be tempted by the dollar bills he had to offer. He was willing to sacrifice the paltry sum that he'd intended to leave as his youngest sons' inheritance to avenge the killing of his eldest. He was waiting in the street, trying to decide whether to enter the Branded Steer, when a familiar figure pushed out through the batwing doors.

Spotting Sheriff Schaefer, Pa Holt became filled with rage and loathing. Schaefer's own feelings showed in his face: deep concern and amazement that the old man was in White Falls on the night after his son's burial.

Schaefer bristled as he saw Pa Holt's intoxicated state. 'I would keep out if I were you, Zachariah!'

Pa Holt spat in the dirt and his eyes were pools of vehement bitterness. 'You and that deputy are right keen on telling Holt folks what they should and shouldn't do, ain't yer?'

'Tate's dead and I'm sorry,' responded Schaefer. 'But witnesses aplenty said he drew first. This Reno Valance is a real quick draw. I'm warnin' you for your own good.'

'That's right touchin', ain't it,' growled Pa Holt. 'I'll go where I want, Schaefer, and you best mind that.'

Schaefer shook his head and slid the Colt Peacemaker out of its holster. 'I'm saying tonight you don't go in the Steer.'

Pa Holt threw his arms out and turned both hands palm forward in an exaggerated display. 'You'd draw on an unarmed man, Schaefer? You know I don't pack a piece.'

Schaefer slid his Colt back and sighed. 'Get away home, Holt,' he uttered in exasperation. 'It isn't worth it.'

'My boy's dead,' barked Pa Holt. 'That's got to be

worth it. My own dear boy murdered by that gun scum and you and that deputy lettin' him get away with it.'

Schaefer knew he could raise the fact that Tate's killing of Nathaniel French's last assistant was tantamount to murder, but he kept quiet. 'Go home, Zach. I already said it ain't worth it.'

Pa Holt moved off along Main Street. He felt the folded bills in the pocket of his jacket. It was well worth $1,000 to find the man who would kill Reno Valance.

CHAPTER EIGHT

'Hell, Silas, this town's wild!'

They hitched their horses and walked along Main Street, which was now a cacophony of noise. Men scuffled on the boardwalks while screams from the bawdy-house balcony drew their attention.

Silas licked his lips. 'I reckon I'll pay them ladies a call. I jest need a drink or two to wash dust.'

Buffett nodded. 'We got to find us a boarding dump with no questions asked. We'll look around after a drink or two.'

Silas jabbed a finger at the Branded Steer. 'There, Jeb?'

Buffett shook his head. 'It looks too lively. We'll find us some place back of town.'

In no time they pushed through the batwings of a rundown saloon called The Springs. They ordered beer and a bottle of redeye and chose a table at the rear of the room. After several minutes of drinking Buffett laid aside his beer glass and sighed.

'Hell, but I needed that.'

Silas swallowed his own beer and shoved the drained glass aside. He reached for the whiskey but stopped short. Silent, they both tracked the drunken sway of a bearded man. The sop lurched toward them.

'Gentsh,' slurred Pa Holt, 'I saw you fellers come in.'

'What d'you want?' barked Buffett. A quick scan showed the barkeep stepping through a storeroom door and two men who had been drinking at the counter heading for the exit.

Pa Holt stumbled. He shoved the table with a leg, making Silas grab for the whiskey bottle. Sliding uninvited into a chair, Pa Holt belched and chuckled.

Buffett frowned. 'You're where you ain't asked, fat man.'

Pa Holt laughed and slapped a hand to the tabletop. 'God darn, ain't that a fact. I'm Zach Holt, goddamn it.'

'You crazy, feller?' snarled Buffett. 'What d'you want?'

Pa Holt reached into his jacket pocket. He withdrew his hand fast, flashing the wad of dollars. 'To offer you thish!'

Buffett grinned. 'Welcome, friend, let's talk some.'

Fitz met Schaefer at the jailhouse. The sheriff, seated at the desk, wore an anxious look. The way he shuffled the papers before him proved to the deputy that his boss was rattled.

'Trouble, Sheriff?'

Schaefer shrugged. 'I reckon we'll both do double shifts for a few days, Bill. We'll catch sleep when we can. Pa Holt is in town and I reckon he's pushing for trouble.'

Fitz frowned. This was a bad sign so soon after Tate's burial. 'Were those boys of his with him?'

'Weren't no sign, but I can't be sure.'

'That's great,' groaned Fitz. 'I mean, as if that hulla-baloo in Main Street ain't enough!'

Schaefer leant back in his chair and sighed deeply. It was strange. His wife Martha, always uninterested when he left to work, had begun to hug and kiss him ahead of every shift, making his passage out of their house a difficult and emotional one.

'Martha's fretting, I reckon,' he drawled at his deputy. 'She's afraid that I might not—'

'You will,' Fitz cut in. 'I'll make sure of it.'

Schafer nodded and grinned weakly. 'I've run an eye about the saloons already, but I reckon we should look again. We'd best start at the Steer.'

Fitz nodded. He was surprised. Had not the sheriff himself professed that White Falls's main drinking house was safe in the hands of Reno Valance? The deputy pondered on the frustrations of the day. All his enquiries into the gunslinger had drawn a blank. The liveryman had given up no clues; Valance's pinto mare was nothing out of the ordinary. Lastly, and in some ways most significantly of all, Anna May could not speak more highly of him.

Fitz vocalized his amazement at that fact. 'I reckon widow Gifford's taken quite a shine to our quick draw.'

'It's a stretch since Todd died,' Schaefer offered back. 'Maybe she's getting set to hitch again.'

'Anna May marry a hired gun?'

'It takes all sorts.'

Fitz shook his head. 'Valance don't seem the type to settle any place long. I reckon he'll do a spell in town before moving on. That'll be the best all ways, I reckon.'

'He's smooth as glass,' said Schaefer earnestly. 'You were right on that.'

'You spoke to him?'

'Not much. He doesn't give up much, does he?'

'I said so,' replied Fitz. 'He's hiding something, boss. But, like you always say, if his face ain't on a wanted form what chance we got?'

Schaefer stood up and reached for his Stetson. 'Come on then. Let's try to quiet this town down!'

'Well, Holt, that sure is an interestin' offer.'

'You'll be willing to do it?'

Buffett nodded. 'For this much dollar I'm willin' to do most stuff.'

Silas reached for the folded notes but Pa Holt brought his hand down hard. 'I got to be sure before I part with this stack.'

Buffett poured out a whiskey. 'Here, Holt, take a swallow with us. What's this feller Valance done to be worth this much?'

Pa Holt inched his hand from the money. He sat up straight, clutched the proffered shot glass and downed its contents in one swallow. To Buffett and Silas the man had altered now. It was as if he had drunk himself sober.

'He murdered my first born boy in cold blood. He left my other two lads without a brother. That stinkin' sheriff and his no-good deputy won't do a thing about it. They're protecting that gun scum Valance and that's how it is.'

'I don't get it,' said Silas. 'You've got enough bodies about you. Why pay us to waste this feller? What's the deal?'

'I can't get tarred with it,' barked back Pa Holt. 'It's got to look like me and my boys had nothin' to do with a killin'. Me and my boys are stayin' close to the ranch now so they'll be no fixing on us.' He sat back and his face darkened. 'That sheriff and his deputy are like molasses on us. Another finger's got to trigger mister high and mighty Reno Valance.' He banged his fist on the table making the glasses and bottle rattle.' 'You got to send that bastard to hell.'

There was silence between them for a moment before Buffett drawled, 'OK, Holt. You got yourself a deal.'

Pa Holt beamed. 'What do I call you boys?'

'You don't call us nothin',' said Buffett harshly. 'It's the way. We need five hundred up top. What's your offer?'

'I reckoned to a thousand.'

Buffett eyed him intently. 'My slugs cost, Holt. It's my neck in the rawhide if you're not in for it!'

'Don't you worry none on that!' barked back Pa Holt. 'I'm in all the way. Two thousand it'll be.'

'More!' growled Buffett.

Pa Holt frowned. He didn't have that kind of money. Times were hard. Duane Drummond's burgeoning Double D spread – cattle raising on the grand scale – had driven beef prices down. The Big B was in debt.

This paltry $1,000 was all the inheritance he could spare to his sons. The ranch was in hock to the bank but Ma Holt didn't know.

'Five big ones,' spat Pa Holt. He would offer them anything so long as they did it. He would worry about the consequences afterwards.

Buffett nodded at that. He dispensed a drink to seal it. Pa Holt took the glass and sipped it thoughtfully.

'I said five hundred down,' Buffett reminded forcefully.

'That's fair enough.' Pa Holt extracted dollars from the pile of notes and pushed them across the table. 'He works sundown to late at the Branded Steer on Main. When it's told that Valance is dead I'll meet you at Stuart's Farm. It's at the foothills – about eight mile north of town. It's nothin' but rubble but there's a sign swings there still.'

Buffett nodded. 'We'll be there. You make sure you are.'

'Don't you fear,' Pa Holt growled. 'I'll be happy to pay if that gun scum's blasted.'

'How you getting told?' Silas wanted to know. 'If you're stoppin' out of town how are you gonna know it's done?'

'I'll know,' spat Pa Holt. 'Law'll make sure of that!'

Buffett took a swig of whiskey and struggled to stifle a yawn. 'I got to get me some rest. You got any ideas where we could set to, Holt?'

Pa Holt nodded. 'There's a boarding dump a few streets from here. This old girl name of Maddy keeps house. She's acceptin' as you'll get. She don't live in and no law'll know you're there.'

'Sounds right suitable,' said Buffett, glancing intently at Silas. 'I reckon we'll head out; we'll book us a bedroll.'

Silas nodded. He downed the last of his redeye and mumbled wearily, 'My sorry bones are longin', sure enough.'

Pa Holt suddenly looked agitated. 'It's jest . . . well, how can I reckon it?'

Buffett shrugged 'What you tryin' to say', Holt?'

'I'm suffering bad on losing my boy,' the bearded beeves man intoned. 'I'm payin' you a hunk of money to kill Valance.'

Buffett shrugged. 'You're paying for a trigger finger.'

'I'll get more.'

'You *got* more money?'

Pa Holt nodded. 'It'd mean more killing.'

Silas shook his head. 'How much more?'

'That bastard who runs the Steer. His name's French. I want him dead too.'

Buffett removed his Stetson to reveal a fringe of hair matted with dust and sweat. 'You're sure in a vengeful mood, ain't you, Holt?'

'I already told you! They murdered my boy Tate. They've both got to pay. That cur Slim Wheeler of Double D should get his as well but I can't risk a range war!'

Buffett pushed his seat aside and struggled to his feet. 'You hate everyone in this town, Holt?'

Pa Holt gripped the edge of the table in his rage. 'How much to kill both Valance and French?'

Buffett replaced his Stetson and smirked. 'You're crazy, Holt, but ten thousand will do them both! Now, you show us where this Maddy's at.'

Pa Holt nodded. 'It's a deal.'

They left together then: two men aching for a rest and wondering what they could make from this half-drunk, half-crazy feller called Holt; Pa Holt cursing the world and vowing to do anything to see his enemies dead.

CHAPTER NINE

They shared a bottle of whiskey in the jailhouse as the town quietened a little after 2 a.m. Schaefer shook his head. There had been trouble all across town again and O'Hanlon's proposal of writing to the Marshal's Service was looking like an attractive one. Still, Reno Valance had efficiently dealt with any trouble in the Branded Steer, and there were no cadavers to lodge in the jailhouse cells.

Schaefer pondered on the saloon's hired gun. In one way, he mused, having Valance in there was just like having an additional lawman. Any problems, Valance would manage them; any killing, he'd be the one doing it. True, as Bill Fitz pointedly said, Valance was nothing more than a paid killer but he was a darned good one and would hold his draw until it was legal.

Fitz broke the sheriff's musing. 'Only way we'll end this gun raging is if the town bans them.'

Schaefer shrugged. 'That ain't happening. I reckon having Valance holding the Steer in check is a useful restraint.'

'I don't like it,' growled Fitz. 'Men like Valance draw trouble. You said yourself Pa Holt was about and angry. It might not be too long before he and his boys come gunning for revenge.'

'Could be.' Schaefer sounded thoughtful. 'But I reckon Pa Holt and his boys know they're beat with Valance. He's too quick and they've seen they'll be six foot under if they ain't careful. Leastways Pa Holt listened to my warning tonight. I didn't see him nowhere so I reckon as he saddled up and rode home.'

'You think we should warn them off again?'

Schaefer frowned. 'No point. The old man will get drunk and shout his mouth off, but they'll tread wary till Valance tires of White Falls and heads into the sun.'

'Let's hope that's soon,' answered Fitz, reaching for his hat. 'I'm heading home. I'll meet you back here at six.'

Schaefer refilled his glass as Fitz left. He drank and pondered deeply. Three days and it would be over. He lifted a hand to his law badge and wondered how it would feel not to wear it again. The last fourteen years, the time had been a double-edged sword. Yes, it brought him authority and status; but it had made him a target for any half-drunk hothead or men with grudges. Too many lawmen died before their time but Schaefer had endured. A mixture of luck and diligence had kept him safe. He and Martha would head East. This wild town would be behind them. The future would be a retirement in New England.

Schaefer forced himself to his feet and, slightly drunk but determined, he reached for his Stetson.

Despite what he'd told Fitz earlier he would ride out to the Holt ranch tomorrow to warn them again. His last three days as sheriff would be trouble free. There would be no embittered beeves family stalking the streets of the town screaming obscenities and threats. No, he would make the Holt men stay well away, whatever it took.

Schaefer stepped out into the cool night air. Moments later, he stumbled down the boardwalk steps and began his route home. Three days until retirement. It was so near it almost hurt.

'You awake, Silas?'

Tyrell stirred in his bunk. He mumbled and sat up. He ran a hand through his hair and yawned widely. 'Dang,' he crowed. 'It's like I ain't slept in a bed for years.'

Buffett was up and dressed. 'Hell, but that old girl was a touch of luck and that's no mistake.'

Silas recalled their appearance at the property the night before. Holt had pointed out her house, and as he disappeared quickly down an alley, they'd roused Maddy from her fireside and struck a deal. After handing over the rent money, she'd given them the key and described the way to the property. No questions, no worried look, just a curt nod and a promise to look in on them after a few days.

'You boys look like you're responsible. Keep the house tidy and no wild parties or such. There's a corral and hay barn out back for your horses. Enjoy your stay in White Falls.'

Buffett chuckled. This was all just too easy. They'd arrived in this flea-bitten town to be met by that drunkard Holt who'd upped and offered them a fortune. With this place to hide out in and no one bothering them, they were set up right good.

Silas interrupted Buffett's thinking with words of doubt. 'I reckon to hightail out with the money we got. It's the safest thing, Jeb. We'll head Mexico way like we spoke on.'

'Stop squawking,' retorted Buffett. 'We're made here.'

'Taking a shot at a quick-draw?' responded Silas wryly. 'Even for that much dollar it's risky. Besides, you heard that old fool – there's enough law in this town. We got to lie low.'

Buffett nodded and stayed silent awhile. Silas was right about that, at least. No, he, Jeb Buffett, did not intend to risk his carcass against a seasoned gunslinger. What he intended was to start a war.

'We got to kill us that feller off the Double D,' Buffett offered maliciously. 'What did Holt call him? Wheeler, weren't it? Yeah, we got to kill us Slim Wheeler!'

Silas's eyes widened as the realization dawned on him. 'They'll put it down to Holt and his boys. Those Double D cowboys will be raging and looking to spill blood.'

'And when the slugs start flyin',' added Buffett, smirking, 'the law'll get busy while we're at what we do best.'

Silas grinned. 'We'll get some dollar. I feel a big payday comin' on.'

Buffett had mapped it all out. They would find some quiet, back-street eating-house for breakfast and then spend the rest of the morning staking out the bank. They'd worked the routine in other towns. As the bank's day ended and the staff left, the manager would secure the premises. Buffett and Silas, unseen, would tail the manager home. They would return later and attack under the cover of darkness.

Silas began to get dressed. He knew what was coming and he trembled slightly as he slid his shirt on. He felt like a man whose fingertips were upon riches whilst he pressed his head against the muzzle of a gun.

'Your progress is quite remarkable, Mr Valance.'

Reno put the book aside and studied Anna May intently. She was a darn good teacher and each day he had come on in leaps and bounds. First, it had been the odd word; now he was completing bits of sentences.

'Why, Mr Valance, we haven't finished that page?'

He aimed a regretful stare at her. 'I wish you'd stop calling me mister; I got a first name, Anna May?'

'Mr Valance,' she responded sternly, 'I find the best policy is to keep arrangements formal. You know well enough that Nat French's assistants don't stay around long and I've no doubt you'll either leave or you'll be—'

'A man needs to get up early to beat me to the draw!'

Anna May's eyes were full of worry. 'Tell me something: how many men you killed?'

Reno shrugged. 'That's my business.'

'Well then, tell me why I would get familiar with a man who can't bring himself to be truthful about his past? As I say, Mr Valance, it's best to keep it formal.'

She moved to rise from the edge of the bed but halted as Reno's hand touched her own.

'I ain't never wasted a man but wanted or earned it, Anna May, that's for sure.'

She pulled her hand away, inched to her feet. 'That, Mr Valance, is the sorry epitaph of every killer that there ever was. There's only one sure thing in life and it's that we'll all die. Come the day of reckoning you'll answer for the blood you've spilt.'

'I told you,' said Reno sourly, 'I ain't scared of hell.'

Anna May crossed the room. She glanced back at him as she reached the doorway. 'Give up this life, Mr Valance, there's still time. You could settle here in White Falls. You could find a new line of work. The preacher could—'

'You're a powerful clever woman, Anna May,' responded Reno, picking up his gun belt. 'But you've no idea how it is with the likes of me.'

She opened the shack door but paused before leaving. 'Please be careful, Reno Valance,' she said softly. 'I worry for you.'

'Ain't a need.' He fastened the belt buckle and slid his Remington into the holster. 'They'll be many a moon till I bite the dust.'

'I hope so,' she whispered as she stepped into the street.

CHAPTER TEN

'You have my sympathies, Rose.'

Schaefer dismounted and proffered the reins to Clement who was leaning against the front wall of the ranch house. The young man scowled but eventually took the leathers and tied them to the top fence bar of a nearby corral.

Ma Holt's face showed her pain. 'Howdy, Sheriff. You'll understand if I ain't my usual self.'

Schaefer nodded. 'I'm right sorry, Rose. But you know what I'd reckon?'

'It don't need explaining,' said Ma Holt. 'I warned Tate and all my boys what would happen. There's always someone quicker to the draw. I ask you, Sheriff, ain't that what all men set upon when it's said and done?'

Schaefer was unsure what to say. He shrugged. 'I was just going to speak to Zachariah. I realize he's taken it bad.'

'We've all took it bad, Mr Schaefer. But we move on. These boys can stay on the ranch awhile. As for Zachariah, well, he's half a bottle from finding himself without a wife.'

Pa Holt stepped out through the ranch house door and his scowl confirmed to Schaefer that the bearded beeves man had heard all of the conversation.

'You can't leave us be, eh, Schaefer?'

'I got a duty to do, Zachariah. You might not like it but I'm required to warn you. Valance is too quick.'

Pa Holt shook his head. 'I reckon as it suits you to have a killer like him in that saloon. I mean, French can cheat all he wants and he knows that hired gun will protect his no-good carcass.'

'If there was any evidence against Valance or Nat French I'd have acted,' responded Schaefer curtly. 'But truth is, there isn't. You know there were witnesses willing to swear to a judge that Tate pulled his gun on Reno. What was he supposed to do?'

Pa Holt looked as if he were about to explode but his wife of four decades ended the matter.

'That's enough,' barked Ma Holt. 'Arguing about it won't bring my boy back. He's dead and gone on account of too much whiskey and trying to prove he was some hard-man. Well he weren't, see. None of my boys are. As I say, Sheriff, them days is over. You won't get any Holt man making trouble in the Branded Steer or no other place. You can let it be known from me that the Holt family will live quiet and peaceable from here on in.'

Schaefer nodded and stared intently at Pa Holt.

'You heard what Rose said,' barked out the bearded cattleman. 'Me and my boys stay close to home now. You won't get no trouble from us, Sheriff, you can be sure of that.'

Schaefer felt a surge of relief tempered with the suspicion of fourteen years behind a law badge. He knew the Holt men too well. The idea that they would now pursue temperate lives on their ranch, forgoing the night vices of White Falls, seemed completely implausible. Ma Holt's face was set with determination though. Maybe the death of Tate had given her a new inner strength to bring her reckless husband and loud-mouthed younger sons into line.

Schaefer stepped across and unhitched the leathers. He was soon mounted and kicking his heels to urge the horse towards the prairie. 'I reckon as Reno Valance won't be around for ever.'

'I reckon not,' called out Pa Holt. 'You mind, Schaefer, that we've got this ranch to look after. We're jest staying here to raise our beeves and that town of White Falls can go hang. We're staying here, Schaefer, you mind that.'

Schaefer urged his mount to a gallop. His last thought as he charged into the distance was that in fourteen years as sheriff, he had never truly believed anyone or anything. That, he pondered, had probably kept him alive.

Twilight came. This evening, with a chill wind thinning the boardwalks of people and raising a veil of dust across Main Street, White Falls was strangely quiet. There was a sense of approaching rain in the air and Anna May pulled her shawl around her and headed towards the Branded Steer saloon.

The arrival of a woman in White Falls' largest drinking establishment would normally have halted conversation. On this occasion, an hour or two before the saloon would begin to fill and with just a couple of customers and the barkeep occupying the place, it produced only cursory glances.

Anna May let the batwings settle behind her before she tentatively approached the long counter.

Walt laid aside a cloth and smiled warmly enough. 'Why, evening to you, Anna May. I never counted on—'

'This is but the second time in nigh on ten years I stepped in here,' she cut in curtly. 'First time was to drag my husband Todd out by his ears; this time it's to speak to Nat French.'

Walt nodded. 'I didn't reckon on you ordering a redeye.'

Anna May sighed. 'It might surprise you, Walter Cooper, but I've taken a share of liquor in my time. I never denied Todd but a few glasses when he'd worked hard. I drink at my own choosing, not when a bottle calls.'

'As you say,' answered Walt drily. Then he frowned. His employer was a man of routine, which he didn't like disturbed. 'Mr French ain't due on till eight,' he advised. 'He's upstairs in the hotel, taking a bath.'

'Room thirty-two, ain't it?'

She moved to the staircase.

Walt was nonplussed. 'You'd prefer to take a seat till Mr French is ready?'

Anna May ascended the stairs. 'No, I'd prefer to speak to Mr French now.'

Walt shook his head as she made the landing.

'Feisty girl, that.'

Walt eyed the thin-faced stranger who had entered the saloon an hour before and spent all that time over one glass of beer. A few tables away another stranger with a livid scar across one cheek also drank slowly. Up to this point both men had remained silent.

'Anna May's a fine, fine woman, friend. She lost her husband that time back and has worked well for Mr French since.'

'She never married again?' asked Silas. 'She's a good-looking creature.'

'You seen she has a will of her own,' replied Walt, struggling to make his mind up over this feller. 'She don't suffer fools and tends Mr French's assistants first class.'

'Is Mr French taking on?' Silas swallowed the last dregs of beer in his glass. 'I'm looking out for work; I'm willing to put my hand to jest about all things?'

Walt shrugged. 'Reno's got the gun role. You'd have to ask Mr French if he wants staff for the hotel. I have to say, friend, you don't look like a feller ready to haul bags.'

Silas laughed. 'No, you're right there. I done a spot of punching; I done me some gun work. I guess this Reno must be good if Mr French keeps him on. From what I've seen this town sparks at night.'

Walt took a bottle of whiskey from a shelf and slid off the top. 'I see things must be tough and you're welcome to this on the house. Listen, we get fellers from the Double D spread in all the time and I'll put in a word for you. They got over ten thousand head and are always on the lookout for skilled punchers. Why, we could have you sorted by the end of the night.'

Silas climbed from his seat and approached the bar. 'So you'll point out these Double D men when they come in?'

'I sure will.' Walt dispensed the whiskey into a tumbler. He nodded toward the still-silent stranger near the back of the room. 'You know that feller?'

Silas glanced across at his long-time partner Buffett. 'Nope,' he said earnestly. 'I ain't never seen him before.'

'Jest another stranger passing though,' opined Walt with a sigh. He passed the gratis drink to Silas. 'Here you go, enjoy!'

Silas slid back to his table, ignoring Buffett and with an eye on the batwings. Outside, as the last light slipped from the sky, the first spatters of rain hit the boardwalk awnings.

'Hell's teeth, Anna May, jumping a feller in the tub!'

'You're decent enough.'

'I am now but I weren't when you strolled in. Why in hell's name didn't you knock on the door?'

'No call for profanity, Nat French, on no account.'

French lifted a cigar off a cabinet and sat on the edge of the bed as he lit it. 'What's so important you gotta disturb me like this?'

'I've got this bad feeling, that's all. I'd like you to set Reno to some other job.'

French stopped his smoke. He shook his head.

'Some other job? Land's sake, Anna May, I took the man on specific. He's a hired gun and a darn ... I mean he's a right good one. In fact, I'd think he's probably one of the best there is.'

'So you won't do it?'

'I won't because he won't let me,' retorted French. 'I'm guessing he'll be as mad as a whacked-at ants' nest if he finds out you've been fixin' to change his work.'

Anna May stayed silent, causing French to frown.

'You can't change a man like that unless he wants to change,' the saloon owner reasoned. 'If Valance weren't a quick-draw in this saloon he'd be doing the exact same thing some place else. I'm right surprised at you!'

She bristled with indignation at that. 'Surprised?'

'You've never fretted over any of my assistants before. He told me you were spending time teaching him to read; I didn't count on—'

'Well you counted wrong,' snapped Anna May angrily. 'I'm just trying to give the man a chance. No offence to you, Mr French, but running gun on your card tables ain't respectable; it ain't right neither.' She looked at him defiantly. 'If Valance were given the chance at a different job I reckon we'd all see another side of him.'

'You're biting at the wrong end of the snake,' drawled French. 'Like I say, it's him you need to convince. I can't afford to lose him as my hired gun, Anna May. With Reno in the Branded Steer I know I'm safe and that's all that matters.'

'And if he's killed?'

French shrugged. 'Any feller who can outdraw Reno Valance is the right perfect replacement. I'll pay what it takes.'

'I ought to say what you can do with your job, Nathaniel French,' she snapped, her face getting red.

'But you won't!'

'Reno needs me.' She stepped to the door. 'I'll get him away from this, Mr French, you see if I don't!'

CHAPTER ELEVEN

Fitz leant back in a chair and sighed. 'You believe it?'

Schaefer shrugged. He had related to his deputy the conversation at the Holt ranch. Ma Holt had seemed resolute about holding her men in check.

'It would solve a problem, right enough,' responded Fitz. 'No more dead Holt fellers littering the cells.' He stared hard at the sheriff. 'Two more days and it'll be over for you.'

'Let's hope they're both quiet.' Schaefer slid his Colt into its holster. 'It took the devil's own effort to get Martha off me again this evening.'

'I told you.' Fitz smiled. 'Nothing's happening to you, Sheriff. I swear it.' He pulled himself out of the chair and clutched his carbine. 'Any word from O'Hanlon on a new deputy?'

'Not yet. I didn't tell you I offered the job to Valance.'

'You did what?'

'Who better? You won't find a quicker draw. He's cool in trouble and a dead-eye shot. He's got all the cre-dentials.'

'The day they take on killers like him as lawmen will be the day to get out,' protested Fitz.

'I reckon some places need his sort,' Schaefer went on. 'Sure, they don't follow all the rules but they get the job done. There's a way about Valance that just tells you he's faced death full-square enough times. White Falls is getting to be one of those places, Bill; I worry about how it'll be turned round.'

Fitz growled with annoyance. 'I get the right man and the Marshals' Service comes through we'll get it done. No, for now Reno Valance can run the rule on the Branded Steer but the time will come when he'll move on, or he'll be made to.'

'You'll make the calls soon,' said Schaefer.

'But you're still the boss for the next two days so it's your call.' Fitz lifted the carbine. 'Do we start with the Branded Steer?'

'Let's start at the back end of town tonight.' Schaefer slid on his Stetson. Rain hammered the windowpanes and he reached for a coat. 'Now I know that the Holt boys won't be about I feel a lot happier. We'll check down Main Street later.'

Fitz nodded and stepped out into the gathering gloom. A roll of thunder broke over the town and lightning streaked out of the distant sky. Fitz buttoned up his own coat. His mind was abuzz with the thought of Reno Valance wearing a tin badge.

Silas saw a man push through the batwings and he knew instantly that it was Reno Valance. It was how he carried himself – a quiet assurance in each step and a face with its features set like stone. The thin-faced outlaw lowered his head and cast a glance back at Buffett. The killer with the scar had his sights locked firmly on the saloon's hired gun.

The barkeep called warmly, 'Evening, Mr Valance.'

Reno halted halfway down the long counter, where he reached for the tumbler that Walt had already filled. He emptied it in one and nodded. 'Howdy, Walt. Been quiet?'

'Apart from that thunder there's nothing to speak of. Oh – there was Anna May.'

'Anna May?'

'I couldn't believe it myself. She upped and came in and went to see Mr French?'

Reno shook his head. 'You know why?'

'She didn't say; just seemed insistent she spoke to him.'

Reno frowned and scanned the room. He noted the thin-faced man sitting at a table near by with his head lowered, and the feller a few tables behind who was staring that way, a hint of aggression in his eyes. These were new faces to Reno. He pondered over the old injury on the face of the drifter at the back and made a mental note of it. He turned back to Walt. 'Those two rough uns been in long?'

'An hour I'd say. Near one's a puncher looking for work and I'm waiting on the Double D crew to show.'

'What about the other one?'

'He ain't said a word.' Walt shrugged. 'Some men are like that. They just want their own company and a table to sup at before movin' on. I've seen it enough.'

Reno knew all about that. Before White Falls that had been his life; he knew that to be hassled was the last thing these drifters either wanted or would accept.

He moved off, climbing the steps to the raised area where he sank down on a wing-back chair. He resolved there and then to speak to Nathaniel French when he turned up for work. His suspicions had been aroused over Anna May's visit earlier and he sensed she'd come to speak about him. When the man with the scar rose clumsily to his feet and walked towards the batwings Reno hardly gave it a second glance.

The thin-faced feller stayed seated, his head still down. Reno sighed. It would be a while yet before the piano player started up with the same old tunes. Soon people would flood into the saloon.

He frowned, his thoughts still mulling on Anna May when a crash of thunder rent the quiet. It rumbled loud and long, muffling the entrance of a group of men.

It was the Double D cowboys, Slim Wheeler at the head of the group. All of their faces were animated, suggesting that they were in high spirits. They spread along the counter seeking service, rain dripping from their clothes and pooling on the saloon floor.

Reno watched Walt pour beers and gesture over towards the thin-faced feller, who rose from his seat. In no time, Slim Wheeler and the stranger were shaking hands and Reno supposed the Double D had a new puncher.

He mused over what Anna May had said to him that morning. Give up the gun work and settle here in White Falls? He would tell her soon enough. He had wandered the huge country for so long, never staying for more than a few weeks in any place, that he had come to accept it would never happen. Then again, he'd never met anyone like Anna May. Despite all her busybody ways, she gave him a sense of inner calm and a growing longing.

Reno's lips curled into a smile. He turned his head to view the clock again as another thunderous explosion broke. Reno flew to his feet. He knew instantly that it wasn't thunder. It was a gun.

Slim Wheeler fell. The Double D foreman cried out and sank to his knees. He held there a moment, hands uselessly clutching at his back. A moment later Wheeler crashed belly down on the saloon floor. A cloud of sawdust rose, hung there, then descended to settle over the red-stained body of the slain cowboy.

Reno crossed the saloon in a few strides. He kicked open the batwings, crouching low as he edged out on to a boardwalk. Main Street was deserted, the rutted thoroughfare and the covered walkways emptied by the driving rain. Water settled in the road, fat droplets slapping into deepening pools, more rain in cascades spilling off the deluged awnings to soak the street's sides with a crashing speed. More thunderous rumbling broke above White Falls, a protracted boom that rolled itself out beyond the town's eastern edge. Lightning struck out – a violent fissure which lit up the thoroughfare with shuddering clarity, no-one showed in that storm lashed street and Reno turned for the batwings.

He stepped back into the saloon where Nathaniel French, roused by the noise, was standing beside one of the Double D cowhands. The latter knelt, turned Wheeler's body over and applied a hand to the slain man's heart. It was a hopeless gesture. The Double D puncher looked up, sighted Reno and his face bore a look of rage.

'It's those goddamn Holts that's done this!' he yelled. 'Well, they want trouble they jest got it!'

'There's no one out there,' Reno told him. 'Whoever killed your feller must've run like hell.'

'One of the alleys,' muttered French. 'They're like ratholes.' The saloon owner shrugged. 'Goddamn it! There're no witnesses, then?'

'It don't need witnesses,' bellowed another. 'You were part of it, Valance; you too, French. You saw it all. Tate accused Slim of cheatin' and when you gunned him down, they said they'd be revenged. Well, they got that sure enough. They'll see what revenge is – every last one of them!'

Reno shook his head. 'We got to wait on the sheriff.'

'Hang the sheriff,' the cowboy roared back. 'This is the old law.' The Double D crew worked together, lifting the body of Wheeler and carrying it through the batwings.

'We're taking Slim back to the spread,' one of them yelled as they left. 'Then hell is headed to the Holt place.'

Reno looked at French. The saloon owner's face was pale.

'Whiskey, Walt,' French spluttered. 'Shots all round.'

Walt poured and passed the drinks. Silas sat there shaking. Though he'd known it was coming it was no less shocking. He accepted a shot of redeye from someone and threw it back. He got to his feet, taking a gulp of air.

'Hold it there!'

Silas froze. He waited, terrified, not wanting to turn and face Valance but knowing he had to. He inched round, fighting his fear. He faced the saloon's hired gun with a look made brave.

Valance jabbed his Remington's muzzle at the table that Silas had just left. 'You forgot your hat, feller.'

Relief swamped Silas's body. He smiled weakly before grabbing the Stetson. 'Thanks for that. I'll be going, then.'

Reno nodded and Silas got out fast. Reno watched the batwings swing for a moment before he turned back to the counter. He drank his whiskey and felt bad.

French noticed. Recovered now, he slapped Reno on the back reassuringly. 'Weren't a thing you could have done about it, Reno. A man who shoots from the dark and at distance is jest a scum-belly coward. He was too scared to show his face.'

'That's right,' added Walt 'Mind, I'm right surprised the Holt boys stooped to that!'

'Death can make folk change,' answered Reno drily. 'You can't ever say.' He shook his head. 'They could have gone for me. I was sat there on the chair.'

'That's true enough,' said French. 'When it's said and done you shot Tate. Maybe you're next?'

'Or you?'

French gulped. He made a beeline for the whiskey bottle.

'We need to get word to the sheriff,' said Walt sombrely. 'Mind, the way them Double D fellers were talking we might not need to worry. It looks like we got us a war!'

Reno strode to the batwings. He stopped short of them and looked back. 'I'll find Schaefer. By the way, I meant to ask, French. What did Anna May want?'

The saloon owner shrugged and Reno knew. He plunged out on to the storm-sodden street. He felt his heart surge. Anna May cared!

CHAPTER TWELVE

They were in the barn, its doors thrown open and all of them watching a storm display its ferocity across the night sky.

Clement spat at the dirt floor. 'I reckon as that lightning's right over White Falls. It's perfect killing weather!'

Pa Holt nodded. 'Yep, I reckon as they'll do it tonight, sure enough. Hell's teeth, but it can't be better. That noise and rain's the right best cover.'

Matthew left his perch on a hay bale and drew his Colt. 'We should've done it. It was us that should've avenged Tate.'

Taking a swing at his youngest son, Pa Holt's fist missed Matthew's head by an inch. 'Your ma's right on one thing: you ain't never gonna be quick enough to face a feller like Valance. Some men you don't go up against. You skin that cat another way!'

'How much it cost, Pa?'

Pa Holt shrugged. 'Just enough, boy!'

'Unless Ma finds out!'

'She won't if you keep your mouths shut, you hear me?'

Matthew stepped to the door and peered out. When he looked back, he wore a frown. 'There's someone riding in, Pa. It's a buggy. You reckon—'

'You two got to learn,' barked Pa Holt. 'While French and that gun scum are being sent to hell I need witnesses to say we was all here. I sent word for Abe and Lara Delaney to come share our meal.'

Clement smirked. 'You're smart, Pa, no mistake.'

Pa Holt nodded. He wore a dark look. 'That stinkin' sheriff and his no good sidekick might think we're behind it but they'll never prove it. You two mind what you say at table. No talk of Tate's killin', neither!'

Both of the young Holt men nodded.

'And tomorrow,' Pa Holt went on, 'When Schaefer rides in to say French and Valance are both dead I'll talk yer ma round. Then, it's Stuart's Farm and this business is finished with.'

'You want us with you, Pa?'

Pa Holt snarled. 'I ain't letting more Holt money leave this place. You two can scoot up by the stream and hide. I want them two fellers dead and I'll get back what dollars I can. I need you both shootin' straight!'

Matthew aimed his Colt at the lightning-streaked sky. 'Don't you worry, Pa. We won't let you down.'

Reno struggled to count the men now crowded into the Branded Steer. Most were armed and all had dressed against the weather outside. The piano player sat on his stool but didn't deign to play. It was useless to try to do so. People struggled to make themselves heard above the hubbub of voices. What snatches of words Reno did pick out were then lost as the storm vented its fury in thunderclaps of extreme magnitude. They rumbled away, replaced by that ceaseless hammering as rain lashed the windows.

Schaefer gave up shouting and climbed on to a chair. He loosed his Peacemaker, directing a slug into the ceiling. A bullet ripped into wood and plaster, showering those below. The sheriff waited then, a thunderclap abating, until he said grimly, 'Men, we got trouble. Right now Double D men are setting to get even at the Holt place. I can't let that happen.'

'Why should we protect them Holts?' yelled back one man. 'They've allus been troublemakers. The way I see it they're gettin' what they've been asking for!'

Schaefer stilled a loud murmur with a raised hand. 'Right now I ain't got evidence on who killed Slim Wheeler.' The sheriff shrugged. 'Short of a witness saying they saw a Holt man pull the trigger it's only talk. I can't have a range war on account of talk. Rose Holt ain't a part of any of this and she could be hurt if it isn't got under control. I'll promise, though, if anyone at the Holt ranch killed Slim they'll be held to account.'

An oldster with white hair shook his head. 'There's nigh on thirty fellers work for Double D. We won't stop that number.'

'If we head them off I reckon to talk trouble down,' responded Schaefer. 'But we need a number to do it.

Who'll volunteer?'

Men discussed it. A few arms were raised. It was not enough.

'Just ten?' said Schaefer dejectedly. 'I need more.'

Late agreement made it fifteen. Those who had volunteered remained, the others walked away. Soon, with the saloon thinned of people, Reno pondered on what to do. He looked sharply at Nat French.

'I'd reckon it'll be quiet in here now.'

French nodded. 'What're you thinking, Reno?'

'It ain't my fight,' drawled Reno. 'But I can't see women caught in crossfire.' He faced the group milling around the sheriff. 'Schaefer, I reckon I'll—'

'No!'

Heads swung in unison. Anna May stood between the batwings, lightning illuminating the street behind, the power of the storm illustrated in her drenched dress and dripping hair.

Schaefer shook his head. 'What is it, Anna May?'

She stepped in, the batwings rattling in her wake. She crossed the floor purposefully, reached Schaefer and shook her head. 'Reno can't go, Sheriff.'

Schaefer stared hard at Reno. 'You hear that, Valance?'

Reno bristled. 'I'm the best shot. I'll be needed.'

Schaefer pondered it. What Valance said was true – he was the best shot by far, but the fact that he had killed Tate meant he couldn't be involved. The presence of the Branded Steer's hired gun might inflame an already fractious situation further.

'I'll use you in White Falls,' Schaefer said sternly. The

sheriff turned to his second in command. 'You too, Bill.'

Fitz was incredulous. 'Like hell—'

'You said yourself I'm still sheriff till midnight tomorrow,' asserted Schaefer. 'I'm still making the calls. I'm ordering you to stay in town and I'm assigning you an assistant.'

Fitz looked staggered but Schaefer ignored him.

White Falls's ageing sheriff stepped down from the armchair and approached Reno. 'Raise your right hand.'

Reno hesitated but then did so.

'Do you pledge to uphold the laws of the United States and protect the citizens of this town?'

Reno stared at Anna May. 'Yeah . . . I'd say I do.'

'Right,' answered Schaefer brusquely. 'You're deputized.' He turned back to face the posse. 'Now, fellers, let's ride!'

'That was good shootin' to take out that Double D feller, Jeb.' Silas whispered it from within the dark of the street's edge. 'But hell's teeth, I thought Valance had got a wind of me!'

'I said they'd reckon those Holts done it,' responded Buffett.

Both of them had memorized the route of alleys between the lodging house and Main Street and by these, following the killing, each had navigated back. They waited a while, guns cocked and ready, tensed against a hammering on the door. It didn't come. They had not been followed; they hadn't even been seen.

The ferocious storm had emptied the town. White Falls was one of those places where, come nightfall, sensible people stayed indoors with their curtains drawn.

Silas faltered then, but Buffett cajoled him. They would navigate the alleys to get a concealed view of Main Street. They would see whether their plan had worked.

It was perfect. Armed men filed into the Branded Steer. A while later some men left, wandering off into the rain. Ten minutes more and another group departed, dispersing in all directions. Silas was panic-stricken, wanting to run, but Buffett steadied him. At last, with time ticking by, men returned leading horses. With a salvo of shouts they mounted up and rode on to the storm-lashed prairie.

Buffett chuckled. 'Come on, Silas – the bank.'

They scuttled through the alleys until they reached the road where the bank manager lived. They crouched in the shadows, drenched and cold. Both felt that surge of exhilaration that preceded all their bank raids.

'They'll butcher Holt and his boys like pork,' Silas hissed. 'Mind, we'll lose ten grand of the drunkard's money. I'm sore to think on that!'

'Hang it!' spat back Buffett. 'There'll be dollars enough in them vaults.'

Silas's nod was unseen. Buffett could hear his partner's chattering teeth, though. 'Steady there, mister! This'll go as slick as you like.'

Silas steeled himself. 'We do it like last time?' he queried. 'Tie them up and take the keys?'

'Nah,' growled back Buffett. 'This is a bigger bank.

I'm guessin' them vaults'll be tough to crack. We'll take this bank feller along. He'll be hostage and that'll mean the bank will get stripped like a bawdy house gal with a ten-dollar bill.'

Silas reassured himself with thoughts of the money. He was still scared but muttered in hope, 'It's a wad of dollars, then Mexico way. Life's sure good!'

A bang of thunder was the signal. It rumbled above, in that black, bucketing sky. They moved swiftly, crossing the swamping road. They approached the house, pausing beneath its sloped porch.

Buffett drew his pistol. Silas did likewise though he knew it was an empty gesture. He had always balked at shooting people. Buffett gripped the gun's muzzle in one hand and rapped the butt hard against the wooden door. It opened in no time, a slight creak sounding as it swung back. A young woman stood there in a lamplit hall. She was no more than twenty, Silas supposed, long blond hair, sparkling eyes.

'Can I—'

Buffett forged forward, grabbing those straw-coloured locks with his free hand and bringing the gun's butt down towards her head with the other.

'No!' roared Silas.

Buffett paused. Then he smirked. 'You scream, little lady, I'll make you sorry you was born!'

She looked stricken with terror but managed to nod.

'Where's that bank feller?'

'My pa,' whimpered the girl. 'He's in the reception room with my mother.'

Buffett hauled her roughly down the hallway. She

pointed a trembling arm towards a closed door and the scar-faced killer booted it open and flung her through. 'On the floor,' he growled. 'Or you'll goddamn die!'

CHAPTER THIRTEEN

Walt and the piano player departed, both told by French to take the rest of the night off. The saloon-owner studied the clock: 11 p.m. and, sighing and giving a resigned shrug, he ascended the hotel stairs.

Reno and Anna May were alone.

Reno nodded at the vacated counter. 'I know you don't figure big on the drink, Mrs Gifford. But maybe you'll join me for a tipple?'

She smiled. 'Perhaps I'll have a brandy to warm me up.'

Reno garnered a bottle from the shelf. He brought two glasses and they sat at a table.

They sipped in silence until Reno uttered, 'I've powerful feelings for you, Anna May.'

Her eyes sparkled. 'I didn't reckon, mister . . .' she blushed, 'I didn't reckon, Reno, that I'd ever feel this way again after losing Todd.'

'I've rough ways,' he responded softly. 'I ain't sure I can make all the changes you'd need.'

'I've chipped off enough edges already.' She moved

a hand out to touch his arm. 'Time will do the rest.'

'I came to this town a man raw to the core, Anna May.' He stared deep into her bright eyes. 'I never got a break. Mr French changed all that.'

She looked hurt. 'And me?'

He laid his glass aside and leant forward. Their lips met in a lingering, passionate kiss. 'French gave me belief again,' he mumbled after. 'You, well – you drained all the anger and turned it into summat else.'

'Love?'

'If that's what it means for a man to want a woman for his wife.'

'My home,' she blustered. 'You could—'

'No,' he cut in. 'Less'n the preacher makes us legal first. I respect you, Anna May, and that's the way it'll be.'

Her wide eyes locked on to his. 'I'll be married to a deputy sheriff. That'd be something.'

Reno frowned. 'Now, wait on there, sister! I agreed to this on account of what's going down with the Holt folk and the Double D. I ain't plannin' on—'

'You'll do just fine, Reno. Yes, sir, the best lawmen White Falls ever did have.'

'Gun-slinging and wearing a law badge got the same risks,' Reno warned. 'Them there slugs are still coming your way!'

'But you'll be honourable.' She got to her feet. 'Besides, you said yourself a man would need to get up right early to outdraw you.'

She walked off and Reno gasped, 'Where're you going?'

She wore a stern face but she was a figure of desirability to the grizzled gunslinger.

'Home, Reno,' she uttered firmly. 'Deputy Fitz will get back soon and you'll need to patrol with him.'

Reno was aghast. 'What in blazes. . . . Patrol?'

'You and Fitz are law in White Falls right now, Mr Valance. This storm might quiet this place down but folk sleep easier knowing a badge is out there.'

She left and Reno sighed. He didn't know where to start!

'What you done with my wife and daughter?'

'Shut it,' barked Buffett. 'They're safe enough.'

White Falls's fifty-year-old bank manager Robert Stroud was horrified. 'If you've—'

'They're tied up,' offered Silas. 'They ain't hurt.'

Buffett threw a murderous look in Tyrell's direction before turning his attention back to Stroud. 'You pull them blinds and set a light or two. Then lead to the vaults. We want dollar bills, mind.'

Stroud shook his head. 'That's the hard-earned money of good folk. It'll hurt them hard.'

'Stow it,' growled Buffett. 'You just do as you're told. Any trouble I'll dress them walls with your stinking brains.'

Stroud nodded, sweat-beads splinkling his forehead. He moved shakily, igniting one of the wall lamps before lowering the coverings at the front windows. He turned to Buffett and pointed at the cashier's desk. 'A door back yonder leads to the vaults.'

Buffett grinned. 'What's stashed down there?'

'It's mostly deposits,' said Stroud mournfully. 'Like I say, it'll bite.'

Buffett waved the gun. 'A slug'll bite worse if you don't stop that whining. What about gold?'

'They're small-time prospectors,' protested Stroud. 'Sure, there's a nugget or two but it's the return a man might make after months in them hills and that's if he's lucky. It'll break them if—' He stopped short and selected a key from a large metal ring. 'Please, if you'd follow me, then.'

They charged into the rain-deluged darkness of the vast land. They rode to noise: fifteen snorting horses splashing their flat-out speed across sodden grass to a crashing backdrop of unrelenting thunder. When lightning struck, forking down out of that black expanse of tumultuous sky, it brought the distance up in fiery relief.

Schaefer heard someone calling to his left. He turned and saw Felix Wilton, a White Falls storeowner, driving his mount closer.

'We need to ride straight for the Holt ranch,' hollered Wilton. 'Just hope we're there before the Double D crew.'

Schaefer nodded and urged his horse in an arcing run that others soon followed. In no time, they descended a slope, the land sweeping down towards that ancient glacial groove in which the Holt ranch sat. They saw the lights of the house, the pattern of its windows casting out patches of yellow. All looked to be in order.

'It's peaceful enough,' yelled Schaefer. 'We made it.'

A rutted lane twisted a route up to the fenced boundaries of house and outbuildings. The pace slowed to a trot, then to a walk by which they urged their mounts through the gallows entrance. A sign swung on chains from the crossbar, its sway incessant in the gusting wind.

They reined up in the yard, the sound of recovering horses drawing a fast response. The door of the house flew open and Pa Holt stepped out. Clement and Matthew, both brandishing guns soon followed.

'Darn it, Schaefer,' barked Pa Holt. 'What in hell's name is this? What right you got to bring this many armed men to my home?'

'A feller's been killed,' yelled Schaefer between thunder bursts. 'He was shot in the Branded Steer not more'n an hour ago.'

Pa Holt, despite the lashing intensity of the rain, threw his head back. Water slammed into his face and he laughed. 'That bastard had it coming. By God, he had it due!'

'He was blasted in the back by an unseen gunman,' Schaefer shouted out. 'Someone didn't have the guts to face him man to man.'

Pa Holt stood straight and scowled. With hair and beard saturated, with rain rivulets streaming down his craggy features, he looked bedraggled but happy. 'We ain't got nothin' to do with killin' that gun scum, Schaefer,' he bellowed. 'Me and my boys been here all day. Right now you're disturbin' our meal with Abe and Lara Delaney.'

Schaefer shook his head. Abe Delaney and his wife –

their farm lay a few miles west – were straight and honest folk. 'You saying Abe and Lara are in there?'

Abe appeared in the ranch-house doorway, which brought an immediate cuss of surprise to each man's lips. Abe stayed in the hallway to avoid the rain. 'Good evening to you, Sheriff,' he called out from the dry. 'Good evening, all you men. Ain't you best get in cover?'

'You can vouch for this?' shouted Schaefer. 'You've been with Zachariah and his boys, Mr Delaney?'

'Well, the wife and me been here for the last couple of hours, Sheriff,' Abe called back. 'We've all been dining on a fine meal.'

Schaefer shook his drenched head. If what Abe said was true, it was clear that none of the Holt family could have been involved in the killing.

'We still got us a big problem,' cried out Felix Wilton.

Pa Holt shrugged. 'You might,' he roared. 'My only problem is our coffee getting cold on account of you lot bothering us innocent folk.'

Schaefer pushed his horse forward. He drew up by the bearded beeves man. He glared down at Pa Holt. 'Double D fellers are headed here to wipe you all out, mister.'

Pa Holt looked stunned. 'What . . . Double D? How—'

'The man killed weren't Valance, it was Slim Wheeler!'

Pa Holt faltered. He stumbled back, his legs buckling under him, but he didn't fall. He struggled to his full height again and placed both of his huge hands over his face. He removed them after a moment and shook his head.

'The Double D crew think you or one of your boys killed their foreman,' Schaefer hollered. 'They don't seem in a mood to be told otherwise.'

Holt threw an anxious glance towards his sons. He turned back, staring up at Schaefer, his eyes wide and fearful. 'So only Wheeler were killed in the Steer?'

Schaefer nodded. 'Yeah,' he yelled. 'Like I say, some scum shot him through the batwings and ran off.'

Pa Holt threw his arms out in the gesture that Schaefer had witnessed in White Falls. 'You gotta protect us, Sheriff,' he cried out. 'It weren't meant—' He cut off abruptly. His voice shook when he spoke again, 'Innocent folk could get hurt here!'

Schaefer drew his carbine from the saddle. 'We'll do our best, Holt, but it depends on whether they'll listen. I suggest all of you lock yourselves in the ranch house. If shooting starts you best get in the cellar.'

Across the yard, the White Falls riders started to dismount, each man tethering his horse and seeking a firing position. Schaefer followed suit. He checked the breech of his gun, sought a shooting spot, and then frowned.

Thunder crashed on, punctuated by Pa Holt's screams, 'You best protect us, Schaefer. You hear? You hear me, Schaefer?'

CHAPTER FOURTEEN

'Anna May's got quite a liking for you, Valance!'

Reno shrugged. 'She's a good woman. She's a way about her to make a man think again.'

Fitz stopped walking. He knew exactly what that meant: Reno Valance was planning to hang around White Falls.

The rain had slowed, thunderclaps came fewer and further between. Fitz sighed. 'You'll see, I reckon that wearing a law badge ain't all it's cracked up to be. Mostly it's like this – you wear boots out.' He studied Reno with a look of bemusement. 'Schaefer said he'd asked you about being deputy but you turned him down. Why'd you change your mind?'

Reno pondered that. So much had happened in so short a time that it was hard to reason. He had gone from a wandering gunhawk to a deputy; from a hard-hearted loner to someone in love. He wasn't about to reveal all that to the deputy, though.

'I'd reckon you'd want any help,' he said testily. 'Better my gun beside you than none at all!'

Fitz wasn't giving up. 'And Anna May? What's she think?'

Reno sighed. 'She reckons it's a step up from the gun in the Branded Steer. Leastways it's honourable.' He paused and glanced down the dark street that they were patrolling. 'Listen, Fitz, how long do we just walk in the wet?'

'We do it till dawn.' Fitz smiled. 'I'll let you check the saloons. The Springs is up there and it'll be closing soon.

'And you?'

'I'll check the stores on the next street. I'll meet you back here in twenty minutes.'

Fitz walked off and Reno made his way towards the small drinking house. It was not busy. Besides the barkeep, the only other occupants were two gap-toothed old-stagers slouching against the counter. Unlike the Branded Steer, this place had no music and the only sound was the men's voices. They all fell silent as he stepped through the door.

Shaking the rain off his Stetson Reno approached.

The barkeep smiled warmly. 'Hey, friend. What'll you have? Beer or whiskey?'

Reno shook his head. He wanted a drink but felt he shouldn't. 'I've jest been deputized,' he offered. 'I've been set to checkin' everything's OK.'

One of the gap-tooths at the bar broke into a grin. 'Hey, you're that gun feller from the Steer what shot

Tate Holt, ain't yer? I hear there's been another killin' in there tonight.' He turned to face the barkeep. 'Like I was tellin' you, Wade, this feller reckoned it were one of the Double D fellers what got blasted in the back.'

Reno shook his head. 'You know anything about that?'

The oldster shrugged. 'Person I heard it from said one of the Holt boys done it; I heard they shot him down like a dog through the batwings 'cause he cheated at cards on Tate.'

'They took Tate's death bad,' added the barkeep. 'Old man Holt was in here yesterday, drunk to the hills and shouting about it.'

It stirred Reno's interest. 'Were his boys with him?'

'No, now you mention it, they weren't. I didn't take much note to tell you the truth. I was out back most of the night, but I did see him speak to a couple of drifters.'

'You mind what those drifters looked like?'

The barkeep frowned. 'One was a scrawny-looking feller. Other feller had this filthy old scar across his cheek. Makes you wonder how he got that, don't it?'

Reno left quickly. He was wondering about it a lot.

A gun-butt met the bank manager's head. Robert Stroud groaned and slumped to the floor.

Disgust filled Silas. Buffett's aggression troubled and enraged him. They'd agreed to lock the bank manager in his own vault but Buffett overrode this with a pistol whipping. At least he hadn't shot him,

Silas comforted himself. Buffett reholstered the Colt and they hauled the canvas bags stuffed with dollar bills up the stairway.

'We done us fine,' said Buffett with a grin.

'I'll be happier outta this town,' Silas gave back anxiously. 'Mind, with this dollar we'll live good in Mexico.'

Buffett frowned. 'That bankin' feller was right about them nuggets, sure enough!' He'd shoved the finds into a pocket and together they'd only amount to a few hundred dollars. 'As big as your fist!' he scoffed.

'Seems digging gold ain't much account,' returned Silas. He'd been just as surprised at the paltry return from the miners. 'Better in this line, and that's no mistake.'

'Still, them nugget tales got us to this shanty,' Buffett observed. 'That's the best move we've made in a long moon.'

'It worked out,' said Silas. 'With the law riding off I'd reckon the Holt place is being shot up this very minute!'

Buffett chuckled. 'It'll be red-hot at that fat fool's ranch. Jest think on it, Silas, he hires us to kill and gets himself blasted. Goddamn fool! Now, get with those bags. We'll lock up, lose the key, then get out quick.'

'Why'd you drag me back here, Valance?'

Reno followed Fitz up the jailhouse steps.

'Wanted posters. Where do you keep them?'

Fitz shrugged. 'They're in the desk there.'

Reno pulled a drawer open and hauled out a pile of papers. He scattered them on the desktop. When he looked up at Fitz he felt embarrassed enough to mutter, 'I jest can't read too well, Fitz. Anna May's teaching me right enough but if you'll. . . .'

Fitz stepped forward and picked up a sheet. 'Frank Leonard. Age Fifty-one. He's wanted for horse theft.'

'It's a feller with a face scar,' said Reno testily.

Fitz picked up more sheets. He scanned the information in silence and laid each sheet aside. 'It ain't here, Valance. There's only. . . .'

'What is it?' barked Reno.

'Well, we get them in whenever the mail-coach pulls through. There might be summat in the sheriff's paperwork he hasn't opened yet.'

Reno couldn't disguise his impatience. 'Goddamn it, man, what the hell you waiting for?'

'I can't open the sheriff's papers. It's not. . . .'

Reno was riffling across the desk again.

Fitz stepped across and grabbed Reno's arm. 'Now, hang about a minute, Valance, you can't—'

He didn't finish. Reno gathered a fist and slammed it into the deputy's face, sending him crashing backwards against the cell bars. Fitz, enraged, attacked back. He dived forwards, and drove Reno off his feet and they sprawled together on to the jailhouse floor. They slugged it out for a few minutes until the fight petered out.

'Darn,' said Reno. 'There ain't much on you, Fitz, but you can punch well enough.'

'And you,' returned the deputy, feeling at his bloodied lip. He moved across to the desk and pulled open another drawer. He took out some papers addressed to

Schaefer. 'If there's anything it'll be in here.'

'Well?' barked Reno after he'd watched Fitz reading in silence for some time. 'What you got?'

'There's a couple of out-of-State notices came in,' responded Fitz. He was reading them but couldn't quite fathom the accuracy of Reno's instinct. The deputy frowned. 'Silas Tyrell, aged thirty-two. Slim build feller. Associates with Jeb Buffett, age of thirty-six. Scar across his right cheek on account of a knife fight.'

'They're wanted for murder?'

Fitz nodded and let the paper flutter to the office floor. 'Yeah . . . and bank robbery!'

Slugs slammed into the ranch-house walls with a rip of splinters and cracking glass where windows shattered. Schaefer crouched in the dark of the yard and prayed that Pa Holt had heeded his warning and got his family into the cellar.

Schaefer waited for screams and yells – any signal that those inside had been hurt – but there was only more smashing glass followed by an outgoing gun blast from the side of the house. Schaefer knew what that meant. Someone – likely one of those hot-heads Clement and Matthew – was fighting back.

'Stop firing!' Schaefer bellowed.

A voice cried out, 'I'll blast those scum-belly Double Ds to this side of hell.'

Thankfully, the Double D bullet volleys had died. Schaefer ran to the window through which the gun had discharged. He pressed up against the wall to one side, waiting. A moment later a Colt's muzzle protruded, the gun barked, a slug flew through flame and smoke. Schaefer moved fast. He stepped over and leaned in, grabbing Clement Holt by his shirt and hauling him out. The young man cried as glass shards caught at his arms, and a moment later he slammed on to earth with a startled grunt. Clement still clutched the gun and Schaefer disarmed him with a stamp of his boot. He lifted Clement, then struck the young fool across the jaw. He let him slump down where he left him.

Schaefer heard horses approaching. A few moments later, a line of riders reined in their snorting mounts at the edge of the yard.

A voice bellowed out and Schaefer recognized it instantly as that of the Double D boss Duane Drummond. 'Any more slugs sent this way and by God we'll wipe this place into hell.'

'Tell your men to hold their fire,' cried Schaefer.

There was a slight pause before Drummond shouted out, 'That you, Sheriff?'

'Yeah, Duane. I got White Falls men with me.'

'You're here to take Holt and his boys in?'

'There's no evidence to do that,' Schaefer yelled back. 'They've been at the Big B all evening. Abe Delaney's here and he's swore to it. They couldn't have been involved in Slim's killing.'

Drummond pushed his horse forward and rode up alone. He stopped his mount near to Schaefer. He remained in the saddle shaking his head. 'I trust Abe's word. Hell's teeth, my men were sure it was down to Holt.'

'They're loose at the mouth and hell-raisers, Duane,'

replied Schaefer. 'But I never took them for assassins in the dark.'

'I guess not,' answered Drummond wiping a gloved hand to his rain-lashed face. 'It looks like we called it wrong. Good job you were here! Still, it means some whole other body's responsible back at White Falls.'

Schaefer nodded. 'Now this is settled I'll ride back and try to track the killer down.'

'You need our help?'

'No thanks, Duane. It's best left to the law. I reckon feelings will still be running high among your boys and I don't want any mistakes.'

'I want the killer found, Sheriff.' Drummond had real venom in his voice. 'I don't give a damn what it takes. You put it round town I'm offering good money for the name. I'll offer two thousand dollars for a name!'

Schaefer frowned. It was bounty more likely to draw the wrong sorts. 'I'll let people know,' he offered back. 'Now, Duane, I'd be grateful if you'd head your men back to the Double D. We'll be able—'

A yell cut him short. Pa Holt hollered angrily from the ranch house doorway, 'Get off Big B land!' The bearded cattleman lurched out, followed by Matthew.

'Easy there, Zach,' Schaefer cried. 'Drummond's accepted you and your boys weren't involved. No point causing war.'

'Get off our land,' Pa Holt raged. 'Leave us be.'

Duane Drummond turned his horse and his men followed suit. The White Falls posse mounted quickly too. In no time, a trail of riders trotted out along the track.

Pa Holt's wrath-filled words followed them on to the prairie.

'We're innocent, Sheriff! You hear me . . . *innocent!*'

CHAPTER FIFTEEN

A check of the bank's exterior raised no concerns. The building was in darkness, its two doors firmly locked and all of the windows intact.

'Looks OK to me,' muttered Fitz. 'Those windows have bars inside and no locks have been tampered with. Maybe those two are planning to raid it during the day?'

Reno shook his head. 'I reckon not. A feller would have to be plain crazy or desperate to take a chance on that.'

Fitz shook his head. 'I don't get it.'

'Who's the boss man?'

'That's Robert Stroud. He lives on Union Street.'

Fitz led the way on a brisk ten-minute walk to a wide boulevard sided by tall housing. A few raps on one of the front doors brought no response and Reno peered into a window. The room within, lit by a wall lamp, was deserted.

'They must be out,' said Fitz. 'We could come back later?'

Reno strode to the side of the house and came across another window. Its curtains were drawn but Reno could detect the faint glow of a burning lamp behind the obscuring fabric. He tried the sash but the window held firm. He drew the Remington then. After grasping the muzzle in his right hand, he applied the butt firmly to the pane. Fitz ran to join him as glass shattered.

'What in hell. . . ?'

Reno paid no heed. He smashed out the remaining glass, hauled aside the curtain and leaned in. He spat loudly then, hauled himself up and dropped through the frame.

Fitz followed and looked stunned as he surveyed the two Stroud women bound and gagged on the floor. 'Well I'll be darned!'

'Help me untie them.' Reno broke through the knots binding the girl's wrists and ankles and she was soon sitting up. Fitz set to releasing Mrs Stroud and both women were soon free of their binds and sitting gratefully on a sofa.

'They've got Pa,' gasped the girl. 'I thought we'd die.'

'They've gone to the bank?' pressed Reno.

The girl nodded. 'Pa took the keys to let them in. They'd have shot us all if Pa refused. It's just—'

'What is it?' barked Reno, more harshly than he meant.

'Pa's got another set,' the girl wailed. 'It ain't bank policy but Pa prefers it that way. They're hid upstairs.'

She retrieved the keys from under a floorboard and in next to no time Reno and Fitz departed in haste.

Soon they'd found Stroud unconscious and trussed in one of the bank's back rooms. Fitz tended to the man whilst Reno lit wall lamps. He walked the interior in case Buffett and Tyrell were still inside. In the vault he saw dollar bills strewn over the floor. The safes were open and empty.

He rejoined Fitz and said, 'They've emptied it all.'

'Stroud's coming round,' Fitz offered back.

The bank manager sat up, a hand tenderly touching the top of his head. 'I feel like I've been sledge-hammered.'

'You OK, Mr Stroud?'

Stroud nodded. 'I've a head wound, but I'll live.'

Fitz frowned. 'You need the doc?'

Stroud winced. 'I reckon not. Help me home, will you.'

Fitz eased the bank official up and looked on in disquiet as Reno paced to the door. 'Where you aimed, Valance?'

'Those two,' snarled Reno. 'I'll hunt the dogs down.'

'You got to rein in there, Reno,' exclaimed the deputy. 'We'll get Mr Stroud back home and. . . .'

Reno shook his head. He left with a growled, 'Jest me and the Remington. That's how it's always been.'

They drove their mounts at full gallop toward White Falls. They stopped once, just out of town, tethering the horses within a clump of trees.

'We'll walk in,' barked Pa Holt.

Clement felt uneasy. It was past midnight and he couldn't fathom what they were doing there. 'Ma's OK with us being out?' She let us be out this late after what happened with Tate!'

Pa Holt dismounted and grunted in response. He thought back to the departure of the Delaneys on their buggy shortly after the mass of armed riders had left the Big B. With Matthew and Clement dispatched to settle the horses in the barn, Rose had set to clearing the table of dishes. She was still agitated at the conflict in the Big B yard and she let her husband know it.

'I didn't know what to say to Lara! We invite good folk here for a meal and we end up with shooting all over the ranch and us cowering in the cellar. I said this would happen!'

'It were mistaken identity, Rose,' protested Pa Holt. 'Abe told them straight we'd been here all the while and they know now we'd nothin' to do with any killin'. That'll be the finish of it.'

'It had best be, so help me, Zachariah,' snapped Ma Holt. 'It best be. Soon as I've finished these pots I want you and the boys inside and set—'

She didn't finish. She had turned away, dishes in hand, towards the large oak dresser when Pa Holt brought a log from the fireplace down over her head. She whimpered, the dishes clattered to the flagstone floor, and seconds later her body crumpled and joined them. Even as she was falling, Pa Holt dropped the log. He headed outside to find his sons.

'Pa! You hear what I said?'

Pa Holt shook himself out of his thoughts and began to haul something off his saddle.

'Pa,' implored Clement. 'What did Ma say?'

'She said it were OK,' snapped back Pa Holt. 'She were in a good mood on account of the Delaneys being over. She said we could spend us an hour at the Steer.'

Matthew stayed by his horse. 'She weren't in a good mood,' he retorted. 'She was raging over bullets and broke glass.'

'I don't get it,' Clement added. 'She set firm on us staying out of White Falls. Why'd she let us out past midnight when the Steer's getting near to—'

'You two calling me a liar,' Pa Holt cut back ferociously. 'I said she agreed and that's it. Now get your guns and move.'

'Our guns,' gasped Matthew. 'What the hell is this?'

Doubt racked both brothers. Matthew's bravado since the death of Tate had now drained away. The sight of so many men with guns in the Big B yard had made him realize that now they were playing a dangerous game with high stakes. Yes, he'd been invigorated by it all as Clement fired out of the ranch-house window, but the cost of losing dawned large and real. If you came second in this game, you were dead. Tate had died going up against a skilled gunman. Those two fellers his pa had got involved with were assassins. It was likely they were quick draws, too. Matthew had had enough. He still had a lot of living to do.

Matthew held his ground and Pa Holt bellowed, 'What in sweet hell you stalling for?'

'I changed my mind. You've brought us here to face those two fellers and I ain't up for it. They sound right trouble; they sound right risky too.'

'You was right up for it in the barn,' spat Pa Holt.

"We won't let you down Pa", weren't it? Well, goddamn it, don't let me down now!'

Clement drew his carbine and stepped forward.

Pa Holt grabbed Matthew's shirtfront. 'Hell, boy, if you don't walk with your brother and me you can get your carcass off the ranch. You're either a son of mine or you're not welcome under my roof.'

Reno acted on his sixth sense. He'd stayed alive this long through its use: a thought, a feeling, a sense of men. One will draw and another won't; there's trouble in that saloon while that one's safe. Go right or left, go east or west. On these things, men stay alive or die. This night he relied upon that sense as he'd never done before.

He inched down alleyways; he crossed bleak and silent streets. As the minutes ticked by, he wondered whether any dark recess could be the place that a death-slug spewed from. He'd hear sharp barks of dogs and he'd scurry in that direction. They'd quickly fade though, and he searched on.

He hunted as never before. He sought evil men not for bounty but because he'd pledged an oath. He was a deputy and this was the selfless service to which he'd sworn.

He stalked on, trawling each alley and boardwalk, growing angry and frustrated at the lack of a sign. Before he knew it, he'd worked his way back to Main Street.

Buffett and Silas, in the cloaking dark of one of the passageways, watched in disbelief as Valance appeared.

Buffett's heart pounded. He'd get a shot at the so-called quick-draw and that was something he couldn't refuse.

The weather had altered now. Rain deluged out, the dissipating clouds allowing an emerging moon to apply its silvery glow to some sections of the road. It was by this and the thrown lamplight of a few windows that Buffett and Silas scanned the boardwalk at the far side of the now sodden dirt thoroughfare.

'Hell's teeth,' hissed Buffett. 'It's him sure enough.'

Silas was exasperated. They had the horses ready for their imminent departure from town and the two animals now waited in the corral behind Maddy's rental property, their saddle-bags stuffed with the stolen bank money. Silas was for mounting straight up and riding hell for leather on to the plains. Buffett had balked at this, growling menacingly that he needed to scout Main Street before they left.

Now the Branded Steer's hired gun was in close proximity and Silas was aghast. He watched as Valance strolled over the timber planks, not fifteen feet away, the quick-draw's gait leisurely and his head lowered as if the man was in deep thought.

'We got to split, Jeb! Let's go before it's too late!'

'Shut it,' Buffett hissed back. He reached for the .44 strapped to his right leg. 'That big-shot gun-whore won't know what's hit him!'

'Jeez, Jeb, this ain't—'

Silas threw out a hand as Buffett's gun cleared the holster but it wasn't needed. They both froze at the sound of approaching horses.

They came in at a gallop, the posse that they had

watched leave earlier pounding their mounts across the rain pools and muddy patches that now defined Main Street. Gradually they slowed, then all reined up.

'Valance!' a voice called out. 'Where's Bill Fitz?'

No reply came. There was no time for it. Buffett extended his gun arm but Silas acted fast. He lashed out, slamming a fist into Buffett's stomach. Although the scar-faced killer doubled up with a shocked howl, he jabbed a finger at the trigger. The pistol cracked out, smoke and flame projecting a bullet into the street. Silas was up and running before the gunshot faded.

Silas tore down the alley and across another street. He kept running, his feet driven by sheer panic. As he plunged into another alley he heard a sound of pounding behind. Someone was following and gaining fast. Terror gripped him. Was it Buffett or Valance?

Too frightened to look back, he drove on, lungs bursting, his legs racked with pain. He still ran, recalling, when he faltered, that last vision. If he ever felt like giving up, he remembered the sight of the moon-speckled Main Street as Buffett's gun blast roared its delivery. He remembered those massed horses rearing with screams of terror. Most of all, he remembered a man crashing from his saddle as Buffett's slug struck.

CHAPTER SIXTEEN

Silas, exhausted and gasping, felt a force smash him off his feet. He cried out in horror, slamming to ground. He scrabbled in the rain-drenched earth, trying desperately to get up again. Something hit him once more, a breathtaking impact to his back that forced him face down to eat dirt. He howled out as a hand grabbed his hair, slamming his face repeatedly into the soil. Grit ripped at his skin and he expected to die. He felt something cold pressing on his neck and knew instantly it was a gun's muzzle.

'I oughta . . . spread your . . . skull right here.' It was Buffett, his words full of bile and fury between laboured breaths.

Silas's guts knotted, fear surging through every vein of his now trembling, aching body. 'Please, Jeb. I didn't mean nothin' by it. I was just—'

'You were just what?' growled Buffett.

'I just wanted to get away,' cried Silas. 'No more killing, Jeb! Let's go to Mexico like we said.'

Buffett dragged Silas up. 'Hell's teeth, I had that gun

scum lined up. On account of you I've killed me some nobody.'

'We got to get away, Jeb,' Silas whined on. 'Riders will be all over us!'

Buffett nodded. 'That posse's back quicker'n I reckoned on. I'm guessin—' He stopped short as a worrying thought hit him.

Silas sensed trouble. 'What is it, Jeb?'

'God alive,' spat Buffett. 'We best hope Holt got himself blasted out. If he's still alive and he's told that posse about us they'll be headed straight for that lodging place!'

'He wouldn't!' Silas wailed. 'It'd mean swinging himself for hitchin' a murder.'

'Men talk with a gun at their head,' drawled back Buffett. 'Come on, we'll hit the grass and ride south like hell.'

They scurried through the alleys. Neither said a word until they neared the lodgings. At last, close to Maddy's place, Buffett muttered, 'You know, Silas, I never did kill me a sheriff!'

'Will he live?'

Reno knelt beside Schaefer's sprawled form. He placed a finger against a vein in the lawman's neck. 'He ain't dead yet but it might be close.' He moved a hand into Schaefer's jacket and felt dampness at the side of the ribs. 'If the slug's missed enough he'll have a chance. We'll need the doc.'

A man reined his horse round. 'I'll go straight over to his house.' He forced his mount down Main Street with heels and yells.

'Rest of you men,' Reno shouted, 'we need fellers posted about town. We ain't got the numbers to cover it all but there's a chance we might catch those two scum riding out.'

'Who're they?' called out a voice.

'Names of Buffett and Tyrell,' Reno gave back. 'They're both for hanging so it don't matter if you shoot to kill. Fact is, anyone riding fast out of town with the sheriff shot don't need much talking to. Let your guns ask questions.'

'You'll be joinin' us, Valance?'

Reno didn't answer. He lifted the Remington from its holster and stepped off into the pitch-black distance of the ambush alleyway. He waited at the alley's end, listening as shouts faded.

He was at a loss as to why Buffett and Silas Tyrell had shot the sheriff. He clutched the Remington tightly and cursed. It would be up to them whether they lived long enough to give him the answer!

'This is Maddy's place, boys. Now, Clem, scoot round the side and see if the horses are in the corral.'

Pa Holt and his youngest son maintained a guard at the front of the boarding house. The fact that his father brandished a single shot sporting rifle shocked Matthew. He'd never seen him with any firearm before.

'Where'd yer get that, Pa?'

'Oh, I had it. My daddy left it me when he passed on. Between that Double D outfit and these pair of varmints I reckon time's come to take this old shooter up.'

'We'll just get the money back.' Matthew's words were full of pleading. 'Get the money back and head home to Ma?'

'Just level that gun of yours,' spat old man Holt. 'I told you before, boy, you talk a good fight. Well, now's time to do it.'

Matthew groaned, tension seizing at every muscle. He shook his head and hoped.

'God-dang, Pa!' It was Clement hissing in the dark. 'The horses are there, saddled up and ready.'

'Get a spot, Clem,' spat Pa Holt. 'They ain't far off.'

Clement tugged at his father's arm. 'Pa, it ain't only that.' He thrust forward a fist stuffed with dollar bills. 'Those saddles is full of dollar. There's a Goddamn fortune on each horse!'

Pa Holt grabbed at the money and brought a scrunched handful to his nose. He sniffed at it as any seasoned connoisseur inhales the distinctive odours of fine wine. 'Boys,' he drawled. 'We just struck us pay dirt!'

Matthew, bemused, uttered up, 'Where'd they get it?'

'They're a pair of robbers,' snarled back Pa Holt. 'Reckon as they'll be wanted in enough places.' He laughed loudly, risking blowing their ambush. 'Get hold of them horses and we'll get gone.'

Clem, confused, said, 'So we ain't blasting them fellers?'

'You fooling, boy?' barked back Pa Holt. 'I ain't fired this old rifle in a hundred years and I'd reckon you two couldn't hit a barn door if you was stood with your noses at it.'

121

'We shoot good enough,' barked Clement indignantly. 'Why you allus got to put us down, Pa?'

'Shut your squawking!' Pa Holt struck back. 'I know you can shoot, boy. It's just ... well, it'll hurt them scum-bellies more now we've got their dollar.'

'They'll be mad as hell,' protested Matthew, panic clear in his voice. 'They'll come after us!'

Pa Holt was silent for a moment, his mind choked with indecision. Then he resolved what they'd do. 'Get them horses out,' he rapped. 'We'll hide them and get back here to settle those two dogs with no names!'

Fitz got back to Main Street to shocking news. While Schaefer lay badly wounded and maybe dying, Reno Valance had set off into the dark passageways of White Falls, going after the outlaws.

As Fitz reached the doctor's office, he saw armed men posted on the boardwalks. Felix Wilton was one of them and he quickly let the deputy know what had occurred. 'We got men in the saddle outside town,' Wilton added. 'Valance reckoned we should blast anything that moves fast in or out.'

Fitz nodded. That made some sense. He'd begun to acquire a respect for this grizzled gunman who couldn't read. He was a seasoned user of that Remington, as Schaefer had said, but he had a command of tactics too. Still, chasing after two men through the dark alleys of White Falls was one hell of a risk.

An explosion of gunfire made them all grab for their rifles. The barks of carbines rent the night air. Fitz dropped himself low, gun poised. He levelled his Colt's muzzle at something in the dark distance. He could just define a shape. It was getting closer and coming in at speed. His finger teased at the revolver's trigger. He was ready. Wilton and another had done the same.

More gun blasts boomed in the distance before a voice, fear filled, desperate, salved their worries.

'Stop shooting, for pity's sake. It's me, Abe Delaney!'

A buggy careered into town, clattering over the ruts of the soaked road and coming to a rattling halt. Abe Delaney sat slumped on the seat while two riders appeared at speed from the prairie. They reined up, looking startled.

'Land's sake!' bellowed one. 'Valance told us to—'

'It's OK,' shouted Fitz. 'No one don't blame you. Mr Delaney's fine so no harm's done.'

The man gave a curt nod. 'I sure am sorry, Mr Delaney. If we'd hit you I don't know how we'd live with that.'

'Like Deputy said,' gasped Delaney. 'I ain't been hit.'

Fitz helped Delaney off the buggy. 'I don't get it, Abe. Why in hell are you tearin' into White Falls at this hour?'

'I don't get it myself,' Delaney returned bleakly. He recounted what had occurred at the Holt place. 'We set off home,' he added then. 'But the wife's forgot her shawl and says go back.'

Fitz wanted to get after Valance, and he let his impatience show. 'For darn sakes, Abe, what're you trying to say.'

'Hold your horses,' snapped back Delaney. 'I've ridden like the devil to get here and damned near got shot in doing it.'

'I'm sorry, Abe,' responded Fitz. 'It's just the sheriff's took a bullet and things are kind of crazy.'

'Mr Schaefer!' gasped Delaney 'Oh my God! He ain't—'

'He's still alive,' cut in Fitz. 'Just about.'

Delaney nodded, saying morosely, 'We got back to the Holts's but it was all quiet. Lara found a back door ajar.' He gave a kind of sob. 'Rose was inside with her head busted. None of the Holt boys was anywhere.'

Fitz exploded. 'What the hell?'

Delaney clutched at Fitz's shirt. 'We need the doc fast.'

Fitz took control. 'Felix,' he said firmly. 'Ride to Anna May's place. She works with Doc and can help. After that, go as guard for Abe and Anna May out to the Holt ranch.'

Felix Wilton was soon in the saddle and he rode off.

A man called Garfield Clayton shrugged his confusion. 'What the hell's occurring here, Deputy?'

Fitz felt bemused. He'd concluded that the shootings of both Slim Wheeler and the sheriff were likely down to these two outlaws. With Abe Delaney's news, it looked like the Holt men were involved somehow. Who had beat up on Ma Holt it was hard to say. He told Clayton what he was thinking.

'It don't make sense,' the other drawled. 'It was Valance who shot Tate Holt. You'd figure if Pa Holt wanted anyone slugged he'd go for Valance first.'

'I don't know!' growled back Fitz. 'I can't reckon it. Goddamn world's gone crazy with killing. And the bank robbed, too!'

Clayton gasped, 'The bank robbed? What next?'

Fitz glanced along the dark street. He felt bemused. With Schaefer dying, the deputy was the lone law on a night gone mad. Yet there was Reno Valance. Out there, somewhere in White Falls's dark streets, the hired ace stalked on.

'You know what's going on, Deputy?' asked Clayton anxiously.

Fitz shook his head. 'There's too many questions right now.' He turned towards the place where Schaefer fought to live. 'I'm just praying,' he murmured as he entered the surgery, 'that Valance has got some answers!'

CHAPTER SEVENTEEN

Reno hunted on. He stopped briefly as the blasts of guns sounded in the distance. The gunfire died quickly and he mused on who had been shooting – and at what? Had the men he sought fled town and from any chance of receiving justice at the hands of a posse? Intuition told Reno no. It was probably the posse getting jittery and blasting haphazardly at critters in the vast canvas of black grassland.

Reno sighed. He thought of Anna May tucked up in her bed: that domain which he knew he would one day share. He felt relief on this night of madness that she was at home safe and well.

At that precise moment, she opened her door. She listened to what Felix Wilton was saying before plunging out into the night street.

Buffett and Silas closed upon the rental with guns drawn.

They too were jittery at the out-of-town gun noise.

'Goddamn,' gasped Silas as the shooting ended. 'Who's that?'

'Hell knows,' growled back Buffett, the gruffness in his voice showing his worry.

'Maybe it's those Double D fellers,' Silas reasoned. 'You reckon that posse's blasting back?'

'Could be,' growled Buffett. 'Maybe after they dead-eyed that fool Holt and his scrawny boys that posse shot some of them ranch boys. They're likely after revenge.'

Silas felt ill. 'Hell's teeth, Jeb. What'll we do?'

'We saddle up with the money,' barked Buffett, 'and we ride hard. If that posse and Double D start shootin' again they'll be too busy to mind us.' He spat into the street. 'I wish I'd been there to see fat man Holt's face as they gunned him down for slugging Slim Wheeler.'

A shout close by brought them both to a standstill.

'You bastards!'

Pa Holt strode into the middle of the street.

'Get down, Pa,' screeched Matthew. 'What you doing?'

'You pair of goddamn whores set me up.'

Buffett was shocked but he wouldn't let it show. 'Not well enough,' he snapped. 'You're still alive, you soaked-out fat fool!'

'We had a deal,' screamed Pa Holt. 'You were killing Valance! You pair of scum blasted Slim Wheeler so that them Double D fellers would gun me and my boys down.'

'That's right, fat man.' Buffett sneered. 'I wanted you and them runts of yours so full of slugs they'd see daylight through your bodies.'

'Oh, you're full of it, ain't yer, mister?' snarled Pa Holt. 'Well, I got the ace of you. We got your dollars where you'll never get 'em back. Anyhow, where you're goin' you won't need money!'

The realization struck Buffett and Silas at the same time. They'd left the horses in the coral with the bank's stolen dollars in the saddle-bags. Holt was telling the truth.

'You're playin' a dangerous game, Holt,' Buffett said menacingly. 'Bring our horses back here quick unless you and your boys want to suffer some.'

Pa Holt laughed raucously. 'On your knees and beg!'

Near by, Clement stilled his trembling hands. He readied his rifle and aimed. Matthew sucked in air and did the same. They fired in unison, that two-gun blast in the narrow confines of the street barking like hell's own roar. A second after, slugs bit into the wood of walls and sent splinters whipping out like the Devil's arrows.

Clement, stunned that he'd missed, shaped to shoot again.

Pa Holt raged. He spat angrily, 'You goddamn fool!'

Silas ran again. He bolted towards the nearest alley.

Buffett didn't move. He burned up with fury that the fat fool Holt had the upper hand; he'd got the dollars. Buffett could see the blurred shapes of the two Holt youngsters and he knew they'd fire again. Besides, their last shots would draw the law in and he, Jeb Buffett, was not ready for a rawhide end just yet.

'I'll see you again!' he snarled.

'Shoot the bastard!' roared Pa Holt at his sons.

It didn't happen. A deafening bang sounded and a second later a slug ripped into Clement Holt's stomach. As the young man staggered back, a blood-curdling wail breaking from his already dying lips, Buffett turned and trundled after his partner. He cursed blue murder with every reluctant step.

Reno moved too. He pinned the vicinity of those gun blasts and got there as a figure shot into an alley. He was set to follow when a desperate cry along the street made him falter. He had the Remington to hand and aimed into the dark's uncertain distance. Something he couldn't define were moving there.

A pitiful wail drew Reno closer. It came again and Reno recognized what it was. He'd heard it before.'

'Clem? Oh, my boy,' howled Pa Holt. 'Don't die!'

Reno heard a clatter to his side and a bobbing light showed. A moment later, an oldster carrying a lamp appeared. 'Say, mister,' the old-stager said croakily. 'What's occurring?'

Reno stepped toward Pa Holt's desperate sobs. The local followed and by the lamp's glow they both saw Pa Holt on his knees, cradling the head of his dying son. Clement's ashen lips twitched but no words came. Then his eyes rolled up and he died.

Pa Holt was bereft, his body racked with sobs, he pressed his head into the blood-soaked body of his second son. Matthew, despair set in his features, stood close by. He looked imploringly at Reno.

'It . . . it's all gone wrong!'

Reno sighed. 'Was it Buffett and Tyrell?'

Matthew wept. 'I don't know who. Pa did a deal to—'

'Shut it, boy!' Pa Holt lay the dead Clement down and lurched to his feet. He'd swallowed his grief, his tears were dried, he just felt rage again. 'You holster your tongue less'n it gets you trouble.' He glared dementedly at Reno. 'Clem's been murdered same as Tate was, gun scum. That's all you need to know!'

Reno shook his head. 'Listen, Holt. I know you wanted me dead and you hired those two to do it. I don't hold that against you though by law you'll swing for it.'

Pa Holt's look was furtive, uncertain. The reality of a noose-end for conspiracy to murder was a gut-loosening one. 'I ... I ... listen, Valance,' he stammered. 'Tate was my first-born. I never meant for Slim Wheeler to get hurt.'

Reno nodded. 'I reckoned as much. I'm a deputy sheriff now and I'll overlook the fact that you tried to send me to hell. I need answers fast.'

Pa Holt's tongue was only half-loosed, though. 'I set it up right enough,' he blustered. 'They was supposed to kill Nat French, not you, but they blasted Wheeler. When Schaefer rode out to my place to say Drummond's people were gunning for my blood I set out to get them two fellers. We came here and got their horses.'

'What's that – their horses?' barked Reno.

Matthew, composed now, spoke up. 'They're loaded with dollars. We hid those mustangs where they'll never know.'

Reno fixed Matthew with a steely glare. 'Where, boy?'

Matthew cast a nervous glance towards his father before uttering, 'Old Fred's barn. It's never locked, and we've hid stuff there before.'

The old-stager with the lamp spat his impatience. 'Excuse me, fellers, my wife will talk me stupid if'n I don't get home.'

Reno tapped the oldster on the shoulder. 'You skedaddle, friend. I thank you for your light.'

The man moved away, the lamp's light swaying as it faded away.

As Pa Holt and Matthew receded back into darkness Reno said harshly, 'Get to Old Fred's barn and stay there. You try and ride out of town, you'll get gunned down for sure.'

Matthew voice returned shakily. 'What we to do with—' He gave a sob.

'We'll be back,' said Reno, his voice softened now. 'We'll tend to your brother, son, don't worry about that.'

Reno turned and stepped toward an alley.

'Thanks,' Matthew called out. 'Pa will—'

His words stopped abruptly, causing Reno to pause. He inched round, Remington gripped and ready. The lamp's dancing departure had stopped. It approached once more. The oldster was retracing his steps. When he neared Reno he sighed. 'I forgot to ask you, mister, but. . . .'

The oldster raised the lamp on an extended arm. Something had drawn him back to cast its light down to where the dead Holt boy lay. Pa Holt knelt and kissed the forehead of his slain son. Then he stood, rifle to

131

hand, and walked forward.

'Don't do it,' drawled Reno.

Pa Holt spat through gritted teeth, 'You think I'm gonna let a stinkin' whore's son like you kill my best boy and live?'

Matthew was on his knees – punched there by his father. He buried his head in his hands and wailed.

Reno's words were chillingly clear. 'I said don't do it!' He paused before saying something he'd never said before, 'Please, Holt, listen to me, for your last son's sake just don't!'

Pa Holt scoffed. He strode on, a finger at the trigger. He drew near and began to level the rifle. Then he stopped.

A blast broke and with a Remington's slug in his throat the bearded ranchman had other things to think about. He collapsed back, slamming on to the damp earth, dead before he got there.

'Son,' called out Reno. 'Go to the barn.'

Matthew was up and running as Reno turned again.

CHAPTER EIGHTEEN

Gunshots continued to rack this White Falls night. They were being fired within the town now, and Fitz just hoped that Valance stood at the right end of it. He knew he would be. That grizzled gunslinger was the best there was. Soon, Fitz and others would enter the labyrinth of alleys to back Valance up. Right now, help had to go to Rose Holt. He heard pounding footfalls on the boardwalk and Anna May appeared. She was panting hard as she got there. She got her breath and stepped down to the buggy. Abe Delaney helped her up into the seat and he was soon clambering alongside her and taking up the reins.

'Deputy,' Anna May gasped. 'That shooting, is it. . . .'

'He knows what he's doing,' Fitz said gravely. 'I would reckon it's Reno's gun.'

She was no fool. Reno Valance was a gunslinger. Killing was his trade and there was something or someone in the back quarters of White Falls that had his quick-draw attention. 'What's happened to get Reno shooting?' she pleaded to know.

Fitz moved across to the buggy and took up Anna May's hand. 'For goodness' sake, woman, there's no time for tellin' now. Rose is hurt bad and I need you to tend to her,'

Anna May nodded but strain showed in her face. She glanced sharply at Abe Delaney. 'Is she badly hurt?'

'She was out cold and not a good colour when I left her,' returned the farmer. 'Lara were doin' her best.'

Anna May looked determined now. 'We best get there as quick as we can.' She glanced down at Fitz. 'You'll go and find Reno? You'll find out what's happening?'

'I'll do my best,' returned Fitz. 'Now, please go!'

Felix Wilton reined his horse slightly down the street ready for their departure. There, twenty feet or so ahead of the buggy, he waited for a sign to go. Then it happened. Two figures darting from an alley made Wilton's horse rear. He fought hard, got the mare under control, glared angrily at the two men.

'What the hell—'

He didn't finish. Buffett aimed and fired. Wilton slumped off his horse, mortally wounded in the stomach. The horse reared again but Silas lurched for the reins and had the animal under control quickly. Buffett walked forward, arm extended and Colt muzzle aimed at Anna May.

'Any man goes for his gun I'll put this little lady into the next world!'

The light from the jailhouse window was enough for Buffett to see the gleam off Fitz's badge.

'I heard shots out of town,' he snarled at Fitz. 'I

suppose you got fellers ready?'

Fitz nodded back. 'We got a guard posted.'

'Well,' Buffett drawled, 'you'll want to let those men know we'll ride out with my gun at this little lady's head. Anyone starts shootin', then my finger might slip at the trigger.'

Fitz said grimly, 'I'll walk ahead till the edge of town. I'll tell the men to hold their fire.'

Buffett stepped to the driver's side of the buggy and, reaching up, he grabbed Delaney's jacket and dragged him off. Delaney crashed into the street with a startled groan. A moment later, mud-spattered and shocked, Abe Delaney climbed unsteadily to his feet.

'God, man,' he cried. 'We got us a woman hurt.'

'You got a Holt boy hurt worse,' retorted Buffett cruelly.

'The Holts?' spluttered Fitz. 'They're in town?'

Buffett was curious. 'Well, three of them were. I reduced that by one.' Buffett frowned. 'That blast just now I can't vouch for. Maybe that fat waste of space shot himself?'

'You animal!' bellowed Anna May. 'You've slaughtered a man and should be on your knees and seeking forgiveness. You'll be in purgatory for this night's work.'

'No, ma'am,' returned Buffett, climbing up beside her. 'I'll be in Mexico. But damn, if we ain't lost dollars in going.'

Anna May pursed her lips. 'I'll thank you not to curse.'

Buffet was perplexed. 'Darn, you're a feisty gal and that's no mistake. What feller's got the lariat of you?'

Fitz tensed. Though he willed her not to, the deputy just knew she would say it.

'It's no business of yours, you vile beast,' snapped Anna May. 'But the man I'll marry is Mr Reno Valance.'

Buffett nudged back his hat brim and whistled. 'Hear that, Silas? We got us the belle of that gunslinger from the saloon.' He glared menacingly at Fitz. 'You tell Valance we'll be at Stuart's Farm at dawn. He'll bring those dollars or his woman here dies.'

Fitz nodded.

'Any posse shows,' Buffett added, 'then this gal dies.'

Silas had mounted Wilton's horse and he protested loudly. 'Goddamn, Jeb, we got to head for Mexico.'

Buffett rounded on his partner. 'You goddamn fool!' He glared back at Fitz. 'Now, lawman, get moving and call loud.'

Fitz walked forward, the buggy following in a rattling pursuit tracked by Silas astride the dead Wilton's horse. At the fringe of the grassland, Fitz bellowed to hold fire. The buggy crashed into the black distance. The last things heard were Buffett's sickening laughter and Anna May's gut-churning cry.

Drawn by a gun blast, Reno got back to Main Street. He found people gathered outside the doctor's surgery and from a quick explanation from Fitz he learned that Felix Wilton was dead and Buffett and Tyrell were gone. Reno was all for chasing after them across the prairie but Fitz cautioned against it. Now, they gathered round Schaefer's bed. Doc Roberts looked grim but he sounded hopeful.

'I've got the bullet out clean,' he said. 'It's a matter of luck and praying now.'

Martha sat beside her husband and clutched his hand. 'He was to retire tomorrow,' she whispered. 'He was hanging his badge up tomorrow!'

'He'll make it,' Fitz tried to reassure her. 'I know it.'

She didn't answer, just gripped Schaefer's hand as if that pressure alone would raise her unconscious spouse.

Fitz motioned with his head and Reno followed. They left the bedroom and stepped down a hallway to the front office. Doc Roberts and Abe Delaney soon joined them.

'Gentlemen,' said the doc, sonorously. 'I reckon we could all do with a drop.' He went to a cupboard and produced a bottle of whiskey. They all sipped at the fire-liquid reflectively.

'I've sent for a buggy to be hitched from the livery,' said Fitz at last. 'I'll be obliged, Abe, if you and Doc can head out to the Holt place to tend to Rose. Posse will guard you.'

Reno shook his head. 'Buffett and Tyrell will be long gone. They'll likely cross into Mexico.'

Fitz sighed. 'I've set men to bring the bodies of Felix, Clement and Pa Holt to the jail; others will patrol the town for the rest of the night.'

Reno laid his glass aside and stifled a yawn. 'I'm dog-tired but I reckon as I'll have to—'

'They've got Anna May!' intoned Fitz.

Reno felt his world turn. The room swam before his eyes, and he struggled to speak. At last, he spluttered,

'What the hell – I mean, how?'

Fitz told him. He ended by uttering, 'They've headed for Stuart's Farm. It's a ruin in the foothills eight miles north. You're to meet them there at dawn with the money from the robbery or. . . .' He couldn't say it but he expected Reno would know.

Reno got control. 'Tell me about the land. This Stuart's Farm – I need a notion of the country thereabouts!'

Abe Delaney sighed. 'Shame Clement were killed. Pa Holt's sister owned the farm. All those Holt boys spent a heck of time about there; they know it inside out.'

Reno had already reached the door. 'Matthew?'

Abe Delaney nodded. 'As I say, ain't nobody would know Stuart's Farm better'n a Holt boy.'

'Old Fred's barn,' mumbled Reno. 'Where is it?'

Fitz shrugged. 'I'll tell you the way. What's there?'

'There's two horses' worth of money,' Reno returned solemnly, 'and probably my best chance!'

CHAPTER NINETEEN

Matthew was in shock when Reno told him about his ma. He sank back on the straw bales in Old Fred's barn with his head slumped down.

The Fred in question was there, roused from his slumber like most of White Falls's inhabitants by the orgy of gunfire. Shooting in town usually died down just after 1 a.m. as the saloons closed. It was almost three when this night's barrel-blasts abated. Whilst most were awake and terrified in their homes, some like Fred and that old-timer by whose lamp Reno had slain Pa Holt had ventured out.

Fred had brought light too, a kerosene burner that he set to a hook in the barn wall.

The old man looked at Reno intently. 'Summat's goin' on, mister! It darn well sounds like a war out there.'

'There've been killings,' Reno responded morosely. 'Matthew's pa and brother, they—'

'They're all dead,' cried out Matthew, looking up. His face looked drained, and though he ached to sob, it was as if there were no tears left.

Fred was appalled. 'Oh my God, boy,' he exclaimed. 'How in hell's name. . . ?'

Matthew shook his head. 'Ma's been hurt. I reckon I need to get back fast!'

'Your ma as well?' blustered Fred. 'Was you robbed or summat?' When Matthew did not answer, Fred perused the mustangs in his barn. 'Where'd these come from?'

'Say, old-timer,' Reno interposed firmly. 'How about rustlin' up some coffee with a warmer or two? The boy could do with it.'

Fred nodded. 'Right – and you kin fill me in after.'

He left, thankfully leaving the burner, and Reno sighed. 'Listen, kid, I had to shoot your pa or he'd have wasted me.'

Matthew thought about yelling obscenities about how Reno could have wounded his father, but then he thought of his mother lying hurt at the ranch.

'Pa must've done it,' he muttered. 'Both Clem and me guessed summat was up when we rode in. We wanted to go back but he made us—' He stopped short. 'She'll live won't she?'

Reno shrugged. 'The doc's with her by now.'

Matthew glanced sharply at the two mustangs. 'There's the money, save for a few dollars Pa had in his hand. Pa reckoned it was robbed money?'

'The bank here in White Falls,' responded Reno.

'I don't know what I'll do,' said Matthew seriously. 'If Ma don't get well I'll be on my own.' He paused then, before spluttering frantically, 'Unless—'

'You won't get locked up,' said Reno 'You've suffered enough I reckon.'

Matthew nodded. 'I'm sorry I said some of that stuff.'

'Threats,' responded Reno drily, 'don't lay a man in his grave.'

Matthew shook his head. 'I best go. There's three of our horses hitched out of town.'

'I need your help, kid.'

Matthew eyes reflected his confusion. 'You're the fastest gunslinger this place ever seen. Why'd you need me?'

'Those two fellers,' said Reno grimly. 'They took Anna May when they rode out of town. I've got to meet them with the money at daybreak.'

Matthew still couldn't fathom it. 'I don't get it, Mr Valance. I ain't a fast draw to back you up.'

'Where they've gone,' Reno explained, 'is Stuart's Farm.'

Matthew's eyes widened. 'That's where we was gonna ambush them. It was Pa's idea. Pa paid to have both you and French shot down. They'd be more money when the job were done. They'd agreed to meet at Stuart's Farm at daybreak, after you'd been killed.'

Reno nodded. It had all slotted into place now. Buffett and Tyrell had reneged on their deal with Pa Holt. They'd killed Slim Wheeler in the hope of starting a range war and during the confusion caused by this they'd attacked the bank.

'Pa were spittin' mad when he realized those two fellers had set us up,' Matthew continued. 'He made me and Clem ride along of him into town to kill them.

141

That's when we found the money and hid it here.' He frowned. 'You know the rest.'

Reno nodded. 'And you know Stuart's Farm.'

'Ain't nowhere in them foothills I ain't been a hundred times,' Matthew answered stoutly. 'It was my aunt's place.' He gave a nod then. 'You'd know that by now, else you wouldn't be asking.'

'I need you to ride out with me,' Reno implored. 'Get me near the farm by a hidden route.'

Matthew sighed. 'Pa would spin in a grave if he was in one. Dang! What'd he say of me helping you!'

'Will you do it?'

'I'll do it for Anna May,' Matthew said. 'We goin' now?'

Old Fred reappeared, carrying two steaming mugs which he handed out. Reno could sniff the generous addition of whiskey. He sipped and shook his head. 'We'll finish this then you get your head down here. I'll be back before light breaks and then we'll ride.'

Reno swallowed the last dregs of coffee and proffered the mug back to Old Fred. 'Thanks, old-timer.'

'You're welcome, mister,' said the old man, turning his back as he placed the mug on the floor. Inching round again he mumbled, 'Now, if'n you'll jest tell me. . . .'

He broke off, nonplussed. The tall feller was gone; Matthew Holt, curled up on his straw bales, was fast asleep.

They were back in those foothills that they had left only a couple of days before. So much had happened in the intervening time it was hard to take in. Jeb had killed four men; they'd achieved and lost a fortune, though Buffett was determined they'd get that back. Silas was not so sure. He was worried as usual.

It seemed crazy. This list of new crimes had no significance at all; they were condemned men before they got to White Falls. Hell was waiting and had been for a long time. No, a gunslinger called Valance worried Silas. He wouldn't just deliver the money and ride away. They had taken the quick draw's woman at gunpoint and that alone would call for a deadly reckoning. Add the murders, robbery and horse-theft, it was likely their violent, hunted lives would end that night unless Buffett would see sense.

It had taken some time to locate the right spot. At first Valance's woman had denied any knowledge of a place called Stuart's Farm. After an hour, it took Buffett levelling the Colt's muzzle at her temple to jog her memory. They approached it in these still, quiet hours, just a coyote's solitary cry puncturing the blank canvas of this highland night.

Silas recalled her name from the Branded Steer as he helped her down from the buggy. 'Miss Anna May?'

'Mrs,' she retorted. 'I was married before.'

'And soon to be again?'

Her face crumpled at that and she began to weep.

'Holster your blubber,' barked Buffett. 'I ain't got the notion to listen to your squawking all night.'

'Goddamn it, Jeb, jest leave the lady be,' snapped back Silas. Since getting to White Falls, he'd challenged his domineering partner like he'd never dared to before.

Buffett snarled at that. 'What the hell did you say?'

'I said Anna May here's scared and her cryin' should lariat some soft words.'

'By God,' spat back Buffett. 'You're a-pushin' at me to the end point, boy!'

'Don't boy me,' growled Silas. 'We should've ridden to the border. Them dollars are gone and you've riled that gunslinger about enough. I've ridden long with you, Jeb, but you're fashionin' rawhide about my unwilling neck!'

Anna May watched as the outlaws came to blows. It was hard to descry the fight owing to the dark. She heard fists striking bone, explosive oaths. She heard shouts of pain as the two men crashed through undergrowth. She heard swear words she just had to ignore. She willed them to keep hitting. She willed them both to die. When it ended, she leaned against the buggy and felt her guts churn as the two men approached.

'Goddamn,' growled Buffett. 'You fight like a wildcat, Silas.' He slapped his partner on the back.

Silas answered through bruised lips, 'Did I hit you enough to make you see what's right?'

'Don't worry,' returned Buffett. 'We can't let that stack of money go. There're enough dollar to buy us the good life down Mexico. We'll be made and safe, Silas. Give this up. No more rough love neither. I'll find me a nice gal and see it all out.'

Silas nodded. 'But Valance?'

'Anna May here'll settle that,' Buffett said with a laugh. 'I'd reckon her and that gun scum'll want a safe passage.'

144

Anna May bit at her lip and stayed quiet. She was as frightened as she'd ever been, but even gripped by this fear her righteous indignation knew no bounds. She thought not of herself. She'd die telling these animals they faced purgatory for eternity in their own fiery hell. She thought only of Reno. They both had to survive. Whatever it took. Whatever!

CHAPTER TWENTY

Matthew grabbed frantically at Reno's arm as the gun-slinger awoke him. He cried out in alarm, calming as he realized who it was. He'd slept fitfully, enduring the worst of nightmares: blood and dying and the world turned mad. Now, fully roused, he recalled it all with clarity and knew the most hellish dreams are sometimes true.

'It'll soon be daybreak,' said Reno softly. 'It's time.'

Ten minutes later, they led the mustangs out of the barn and into the hushed town.

Reno got just two hours' sleep. Having left the barn, he'd checked on Schaefer, who was still unconscious with his wife beside him. Doc Roberts had not returned. It was an ominous sign that Rose Holt was gravely injured. He'd shared a quick whiskey with Fitz in the sheriff's office, pausing only to consider the bodies arranged on the cell floor. He'd hit his bed in the shack then, crashing down on to it like someone blasted by a slug at close range.

Fitz had agreed to stay awake; he would rouse Reno

after the two hours. The posse had been stood down and after many had paid their respects to the slain men, they'd drifted off to their homes.

Right then, Reno supposed, no one would be awake.

'Mr Valance.'

They'd cleared the edge of town and were preparing to climb into the saddle.

'What is it, kid?'

'I want one thing back; one thing for helping you.'

'Don't say it, kid.' Reno shook his head. 'Don't ask me to teach you to quick-draw!'

'Goddamn it,' protested Matthew. 'You don't get this chance but once in a life.'

'Gunslingers don't deal in life, kid. It's always the other end. They call me Ace on account I deal only in death.'

'You'll show me?'

Reno sighed. 'I ain't sure. When this is over, when I've got my head right and sorted things with Anna May, I reckon you can ask me again.'

This time Matthew grabbed at Reno's arm. 'You'll teach me?'

'Maybe, kid, just maybe.'

Matthew clutched the reins and dug his spurs in. 'We'll do this, Mr Valance,' he shouted as his horse bolted on. 'We'll get Anna May safe and those fellers dead and I'll be taught fast as lightnin'.'

Reno urged his mustang on. He yearned for Anna May. There was something else though; for the first time since childhood he felt fear. A beating from a drunkard with a hemp rope when he'd been aged nine;

the death of his mother a year after; now the thought of losing the only thing he'd ever loved during his blood-soaked life. It felt the same right now. It was punishing and produced pain that felt unbearable.

They slept, Silas giving up the bedroll from the stolen horse to Reno's wife-to-be. Buffett stayed awake, Colt in his hand, hammer cocked. He chose a rock and sat gazing out into the blackness, just waiting for the first hint of light.

During the seemingly endless hours to dawn, Buffett's mind ran firstly on the loot from the bank, then on Reno Valance. He knew the gun slick would come, and someone who drew as fast as he did would not be afraid to confront them face to face. Buffett had drawn against many men and left most dead. Yet he'd never been a gunslinger; he'd always sought to avoid them. He would not run this time though. Reno Valance had the fortune with which he and Silas would live the remainder of their lives in Mexican comfort. They had something, Buffett reckoned, more valuable than money to that man who packed a Remington in the Branded Steer saloon. They'd seek to barter. It would be dollars for a life.

When day came, it lit the grey mist drifting through the trees. Buffett pushed himself up from the rock and he shivered. The night had been cold. It was still bitter now. Normally Buffett would figure a fire but right then, he resisted it. He longed for coffee – steaming hot. He longed even more for whiskey.

He walked, his boot souls crushing a scattering of

windfall. It was wet from the rain but crunched enough underfoot to rouse Silas and Anna May. They both struggled up.

Silas yawned and stamped his feet hard to engender some feeling in them. 'Goddamn,' he growled. 'It's colder than a. . . .' He trailed off, glancing sharply at Anna May.

Her look was a mixture of displeasure and fear. While her face betrayed a woman angered, her eyes disclosed her deep worry.

Buffett moved off on foot to scout through the trees. He located the ruins of the farm: only a few low courses of stone remaining as evidence of where the house had been. Yet, as Pa Holt had said, a wooden sign in reasonable condition still hung on a crossbar supported by two stout posts. Behind the ruins the land climbed sharply as a stepped cliff of rock, partly colonized by scrub. To the left, maybe 200 yards away there were more trees. Only the land ahead of the ruins was flat and open. It was here, Buffett supposed, that the farm owners had kept cattle. It was across this that Reno Valance would almost certainly come.

Buffett started to turn when something caught his attention. It was a dot in the distance but to a man versed in scanning for posses it was enough. He just knew – he sensed it – that men were riding towards him and they were moving fast.

'Silas!' he bellowed.

Moments later, his partner appeared accompanied by Anna May. She'd considered remaining where she was, even of running the moment Silas disappeared through the trees, but the thought that Reno was approaching made her follow the thin outlaw. When they got there, Buffett jabbed a finger at the horizon.

'What d'you reckon?'

Silas squinted and then shrugged. 'It's riders sure enough. I wouldn't reckon it to be a posse. There ain't enough. I'd reckon three.'

'You get out of sight with your lady friend,' growled Buffett. 'Jest thumb that gun.'

Silas nodded, and he and Anna May hid behind some creosote scrub.

In no time, the drumming of hoofs signalled the arrival of three mounted men. They were all breathing hard in the saddle as they surveyed Buffett.

'Say, feller,' called out one, 'can you point us the way to White Falls?'

'What's your business there?' returned Buffett warily.

The man shrugged. 'We ain't sure yet. We heard there's been gold found and where there's nuggets there's allus a way to profit.'

Buffett shook his head. 'Dang, if that ain't what I reckoned to myself. Trouble is, boys, I'm in a bad way and a gunslinger comin', too.'

One of the men shrugged. 'What in hell're you jawin' about, mister?'

'I just got to know if I'm quick enough,' Buffett growled back. 'You allus ask yourself. Can I take him?'

They stiffened in their saddles. 'Just say where, feller,' snarled the rider. 'White Falls is the place.'

'I'll tell you what you'll do,' baited Buffett. 'You'll turn your horses and ride back to which ever bitch-flabby whores brought you into this world.'

Their faces tightened. Their eyes narrowed with doubt and anger. Their fingers twitched at the reins.

Silas shot out of hiding. He knew what was coming and he wanted no more. 'Listen, fellers,' he cried. 'There ain't any point in this. You all set south about eight miles.'

It was too late. Buffett's hand had closed on the butt of his Colt.

Though silence reigned, it was a quiet that shouted with fear and anger. Who would go first? Who would dare to test the nerve and speed of another?

One of the riders broke first. He lunged for his sidearm but Buffett threw up his Colt and flat palmed the hammer in one swift move. The muzzle spewed death, a slug slamming into the target's chest. He crashed backwards off his horse to lie as a crumpled corpse on the grass.

A second rider sought escape. He dragged his mount around and raked spurs to her flanks. She bolted and made ground.

The third rider held. He sat upright in the saddle with his hands up. He surveyed the remains of his dead friend and shook his head.

'You killed Cal,' he gasped. 'We jest wanted to. . . .'

Buffett edged forward and smiled. 'You jest . . .' He depressed the trigger and sent a slug into the man's forehead, '. . . wanted to die!'

The fleeing rider had almost made it. A few feet more and he'd be beyond pistol range. He'd got the horse under him into a weaving run. He glanced back once, his face breaking into a look of triumph.

Buffett levelled the Colt and snarled. 'Goddamn it. Some folk never learn.' He pressed the trigger and watched with satisfaction as the horse spun off its feet and fell in a flailing of legs and frantic screams. The rider crashed off, his horse rearing across his legs.

Buffett got there to find a man in pain. The wounded horse pinioned him down and the beast was dying slow.

The man beneath pleaded through gritted teeth. 'My leg's busted.'

'I'm worried about that animal,' growled Buffett.

The trapped man spat, 'She's sufferin', goddamn it.'

Buffett nodded and aimed the Colt again. 'I need to put it out of its misery.' He levelled the gun at the distressed animal but then trained it on the man. 'But first it's got to be you!'

Two gun blasts signalled the end and Silas sprinted forward, stunned into silence. He surveyed the carnage all around the prairie and it all seemed surreal.

'You goddamn fool,' he raged at Buffett. 'When will it end?'

Reno and Matthew had watched in disbelief. The surviving Holt boy had guided Reno through pitch darkness to a site above the farm. The horses, tethered to a cottonwood branch, both reared as the gun blasts barked. As silence settled again, the animals grew quieter and Reno slammed a fist at the ground.

'That man's crazy,' he growled. 'We got to get down there before he does something to Anna May.'

Matthew nodded. 'If we leave the horses here there's a quick way.'

In no time, they'd descended the cliff by way of an unseen and naturally hewn path and were closing on the farm ruins. Reno studied the scene. Buffett and Silas, progressing back from the prairie with loud and angry voices were closing on Anna May who'd risen from her creosote cover and stood, shawl wrapped tightly about her, against the buggy.

'You stay here,' Reno hissed to Matthew. 'This is between me and them.'

'Like hell,' gasped Matthew vehemently. 'They killed my brother. You reckon as—'

Reno's hand cloaked his mouth. 'OK. Just do as I say.'

Matthew's eyes were wide and he nodded. He raised the Colt .45 and clicked back the hammer. 'I'm ready!'

'Keep your eyes fixed on that thin feller, Tyrell,' Reno instructed in a whisper. 'Never take your sight off him. I've got Buffett and if you get distracted it could cost our lives!'

Matthew nodded but he was trembling. 'The thin one?'

'No matter what's said or done, don't take your eyes or that gun off Tyrell!'

'I hear you, Mr Valance.'

'Now,' said Reno sombrely, 'let's get it done!'

CHAPTER TWENTY-ONE

Buffett and Silas were back. They drew near to Anna May but checked as Reno and Matthew stepped into view. Anna May gasped, Silas looked fear-stricken. Buffett just smirked.

The scar-faced killer jabbed a finger at the carnage he'd caused. 'I reckon you've seen what I can do?'

Matthew clamped his gaze to Silas Tyrell. The thin outlaw didn't move, hand frozen over his gun butt.

'Oh, I've seen what you do, all right,' returned Reno bitterly. 'You kill for no reason; you beat up on anyone; you rob what ain't yours. You've got one big problem, feller, and I aim to fix it.'

Buffett shook his head. He raised his arm to direct his Colt at Anna May. 'I got two left.'

Reno had counted. Buffett had used two slugs on the near riders; two more to end the life of the man who'd fled and his injured mare. 'You got one,' he drawled. 'You ain't packin' six in that chamber unless you're crazier than I thought.'

'It don't matter much,' Buffett gave back. 'She'll die, gun-slick, unless you bring our money and then back off.'

Anna May forced herself to her full height and she breathed in deeply. She spoke, giving vehemence to her words. 'I ain't afraid to die. My soul's clear and heaven awaits me. You two, on the other hand, will burn for eternity.'

Buffett laughed. 'I wouldn't reckon there's too much redeye in heaven. No bawdy gals neither. Why anyone would want it, I just don't get.'

Anna May gave out then. The accumulated stress and fear she'd endured through this night had become too much and she sobbed uncontrollably. Silas twitched as she wept. He remembered the clean handkerchief in his back pocket. He reached for it, an act of consideration if not kindness, but it began the end.

Matthew was as taut as wire. His eyes hadn't left the thin outlaw for a second and when Silas's hand shifted the Holt boy fired. The gun blazed, spitting cordite and fire, and a slug ripped into flesh.

'Hell's teeth,' cried Matthew. 'I sank the sucker!'

As the bullet struck Silas staggered backwards, his hands clutching pathetically at his blood-soaked midriff. He dropped to his knees, groaned, and died in a heap.

Reno stepped forward, primed to fire, but the woman he yearned for was in his way. He watched in horrified silence as Anna May launched at Buffett. She slammed into the outlaw, driving him sideways. Despite Anna May's weight knocking his arm, Buffett got off a shot. His Colt coughed out its deadly load and as he sprawled to the ground, the slug intended for Reno

155

tore into Matthew Holt.

The young man screamed, a searing pain gripping his shoulder. He dropped his gun and slumped down.

Reno's finger itched at the trigger but he could not shoot. Ahead of him, Buffett and Anna May were on the ground and struggling like wildcats.

Buffett triumphed. He thrust out a hand and grabbed Anna May's hair. She screamed as Buffett dragged her up, forcing her forward as a shield. He stood behind her and snarled, 'Now, gun-slick, you stay steady there.'

He backed away, hauling Anna May with him, making for Silas's body.

'Let her go,' gritted Reno with menace in his voice.

'God alive,' returned Buffett, bending his knees to reach down and collect Silas's spilled Colt. 'I got the score of you, Valance. I see how it is, right enough.' His fingers closed round the butt of Silas's gun and, armed again, he rose back to full height. He gave a snort of indignation. 'If you want to jump the broom with this bitch you best get that money and bring it here.'

Reno growled, 'Even scum like you don't shoot women.'

'I'll do what I got to do to get my money,' spat back Buffett. 'I got the top hand here. There ain't no beatin' it.'

'You ain't got the ace,' returned Reno with fire in his eyes. 'That belongs to me.'

Buffett looked unsure. 'I'll kill this bitch, Valance. Now, don't be pressin' me no more!'

'Do it,' spat Reno. 'And folks'll tell their young how some scum called Buffett couldn't stand up, gun to gun.

He had him a woman as a shield and it was she he killed.'

Buffett shook his head. 'They say you're fast.'

'Ain't no one quicker.'

Buffett glared at the dead body of his partner. He muttered regretfully, 'I've got this anger in me, Valance. You savvy that?'

'I've been there,' returned Reno. 'But you've gone where no man can live, and you need to leave.'

'To hell?'

'It's over,' said Reno. 'You choose how you go.'

'Fast and famous,' said Buffett with a smile. 'Me and the quick-draw and they'll say I went down fightin'.' Buffett sighed. 'I'm darned quick myself, Valance. You willin' to take that risk?'

Reno said solemnly, 'The kid knows where the money's at.'

Buffett shoved Anna May aside. He slid Silas's Colt into his holster and shook his head. 'So this is it?'

'It comes to us all – sometime.'

'Fast and famous,' intoned Buffett lunging for his gun. It was the last thing he ever said. Someone wrote, later, that Reno got him between the eyes from near on ninety feet.

Bill Fitz served coffee in the sheriff's office. Drinks handed out, he sank into his chair and shook his head. 'Who those three fellers were I jest don't know. There was nothin' on their bodies to say.'

'Jest drifters then?'

Fitz studied Reno intently and nodded. 'Just fellers headed for White Falls, looking for a gain.'

157

Reno squeezed Anna May's hand and, seated as they were, side by side, she was able to lean across and respond with a kiss.

'I take it,' said Fitz with a grin. 'It won't be long before you pair get hitched.'

They disengaged from their passion and Anna May nodded. 'With Reno as a deputy sheriff we'll—'

'Now, stay it a minute, sister,' protested Reno. 'I done this tin star lark on account of—'

'No, you'll be a deputy sheriff of White Falls, Mr Valance,' she cut back. 'That's my final word on it!'

Reno shrugged and sagged back in his chair.

'I don't reckon you'll be needed in the Branded Steer,' Fitz contributed. 'Since that night of killing most of the drifters and rough riders have hightailed it out. You turned this town about, Reno and we got a lot to be grateful on!'

The office door was open and above the hum of midday voices as people strode the boardwalk, a sudden clattering told them the buggy had arrived.

Fitz slid open a desk drawer and pulled out a bundle wrapped in brown paper. 'I got it from the bank first thing.' He wore a look of huge satisfaction now. 'I'd reckon it'll get your wedded arrangements off to a good start.'

Anna May leaned forward and took the bounty. 'How much is here, Sheriff Fitz?'

'Five thousand from the bank for recovering their money; then there's another three for takin' down Buffett and Tyrell.'

Anna May climbed to her feet. 'Come along, Mr

Valance, we've got a ride to take.'

'Be here for the day shift tomorrow,' called out Fitz
as he watched them go. He leant back in his seat and
shook his head. With Reno Valance around, he just
knew everything would turn out fine.

They crossed those few miles of prairie to the Holt ranch.
Now, under strong but pleasant sunshine, Ma Holt sat in
a rocking chair outside the front door whilst near by her
youngest son, his right arm in a sling, was doing his best
to lariat a calf in one of the pens. Matthew let the rope
drop and he wandered across to his mother.

Reno stopped the buggy and assisted Anna May
down.

'Matthew,' said Ma Holt immediately. 'Bring two
chairs.'

The youngster went towards the door but Reno beat
him to it. He'd soon brought out the seating from the
ranch-house kitchen.

'I've a drop of best brandy if you're in that frame of
thinking,' Ma Holt declared.

Reno shook his head. 'We just came to see you're OK
– both you and the boy there, Mrs Holt.'

Ma Holt nodded. 'As well as we can be when most
your family's gone. Still, Zachariah got what he had
comin' I'd reckon right enough.' She did her best to
smile. 'Sheriff Schaefer?'

'He'll recover,' Anna May stated. 'He's bound for
Boston with Martha as soon as he's well. They've sold
their home.'

Ma Holt gazed wistfully around. 'It's hard to leave the

place you've known. This has been my home for nigh on thirty years. All my boys got born here.' She sighed then. 'Guess me and Matthew will get used to a new place.'

'We reckoned it would be tough now,' Anna May said.

'One boy can't run a place this size,' Ma Holt answered sombrely, 'much as he'd try. We jest can't afford to take men on. I'd reckon we might—'

Anna May thrust the bundle forward. Ma Holt took it with a trembling hand. Slowly she peeled the paper and her eyes moistened. 'This is a right lot of money,' she said with jerky words. 'With this we could hire on. We might make it.'

Reno stood up and took Anna May's hand. 'Shall we, my love?'

Anna May glanced up at the clear blue skies. 'An hour or two only, mind. I don't want you catching the sun.'

Reno pushed back the brim of his hat and shook his head. 'Lady, you've a pushin' way and that's no mistake.'

'I know,' she grinned. 'You've told me that before.'

Seated on the buggy, Reno picked up the reins and prepared to move the horse on.

'Where'd it come from?' called out Matthew. 'All that money you gave Ma?'

'It's bounty,' responded Reno with a wink of his eye. 'It's what us gunslingers call dead-eye dollar.'

'You'd give all that?' Matthew gasped. 'All your reward money?'

Reno raised his hat to Ma Holt and flicked at the reins. The buggy moved off in a slow trundle towards the prairie. He gazed lovingly at Anna May as he shouted back, 'I got me the best reward of all!'